DEAD BANGKOK

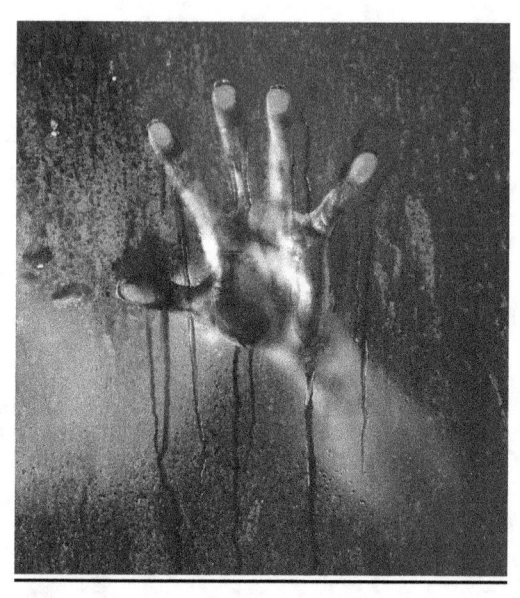

DEAD BANGKOK

A Novel of Thailand

J.D. VILLINES

BEACHFRONT PRESS

Los Angeles, California

ISBN-13: 978-0615514543

ISBN-10: 0615514545

Contact: beachfrontpress@yahoo.com

Prologue

Ours is a long, slow suicide. Life metered out in milligrams and bullets. Parasites and hosts. An ecosystem of the absurd. Marbleized veins ran up his legs into a spider web of blue on his stomach. The veins stretched out across his chest and back, viewed through the sheen of translucent skin. *Onchocerca volvulus* parasites multiplied inside of him. His body, a host to competing parasitic colonies. He examined his eyes in the mirror. He could see them swimming in his ocular fluid. There was only one known cure: To sterilize the parasites so they couldn't reproduce. This meant he would only have to wait ten years before they left his body.

He looked down at his leg. He could see the bump where the Guinea worm was emerging. It had crippled him as it worked its way out. When the blister formed, he took a bath and watched as it popped, to release the hundred or so thousand larvae into the water. Now the female was emerging. It would take several weeks for the noodle-shaped parasite to fully work its way out. He tied a string around what he presumed to be its head, and the other end to a chopstick. Over the coming weeks, Esmeralda would roll the worm around the stick until it had completely emerged. He planned on giving it as a gift to someone. He had already saved the bathwater with the larvae in it, bottling it inside some Evian. He snapped new safety caps on the bottles and placed them in his fridge, which by now had become his own bio-weapons lab.

Esmeralda tucked his genitals between his thighs and looked in the mirror. He needed breasts to pull off the look. He donned his wig and applied his makeup. The Adam's apple would have to go, too. All in all, he was looking at about twenty grand to complete his transformation. For now, this would have to work. Esmeralda danced around the room to the nauseating girlie pop music he thought a woman would dance to. He affected femininity with all the grace of a showgirl suffering from an inner-ear infection. It was nearly hopeless.

Esmeralda's text message sounded.

Ekamai bus station – 21:00

He looked in the mirror again. He was doing its bidding. The ever-evolving parasites in his brain were now controlling his behavior From now on, there could be no sin. No culpability. No existential self to fret over. For now, he did as the parasite ordered.

The .45 and shotgun were under the bed. He loaded them with frangible rounds – the ones that, for lack of a better word, *exploded* inside the victim. Douse the corpses with gasoline, he was told, and remove the hands and head for good measure. Forensic teams can be so thorough these days.

Esmeralda took his estrogen pills and changed back into those other clothes – the unnatural and manly ones that made him feel so outside of himself. His computer played footage of the Juba sniper in Baghdad. It was a greatest-hits compilation. Juba was a myth. An urban legend. The footage of American soldiers dropping like flies to Juba's bullets was simply the work of many snipers. All of it packaged and sold to the Arab world as the new Vasily Zaytsev. Esmeralda admired the fear that Juba created, and it was his legend that left Esmeralda inspired. Esmeralda had failed in all of his attempts at joining the military. He got as far as MEPS and when he was asked to pick a job, he told the man behind the desk that he wanted to work where they kept the alien bodies. The ones he saw on TV. The ones they kept in an underground bunker or lab. *We don't have any alien bodies,* the man replied. Esmeralda looked into the man's eyes. He could see them swimming in his ocular fluid as well. He knew they would soon be inside of everyone.

This job called for a reversible jacket, and quick-change disguise kit that had been left for him in a dead-drop. Esmeralda opened the large manila envelope and looked inside. It was a bad toupee lined with solenoids. They had redesigned the machine into a covert model. It was now hidden inside a hairpiece that resembled a bad comb-over. It would induce a form of temporal lobe epilepsy that allowed him to communicate with the parasites in his brain. Its only side effects were visions of hell. They had chosen him out of all of the test subjects because he was the only one that could wear the machine for an extended period of time. After only a few minutes, it had driven the other candidates insane. Esmeralda looked in the mirror and adjusted the toupee. He always thought of himself as more of a blonde. Someone famous like a Paris Hilton impersonator. Someday, he swore that he would pay her a visit and scalp her, and make a wig out of her actual hair. Then he would set fire to her little rat dog and laugh while it ran around in circles

Esmeralda's apartment was in Khlong Toey section of Bangkok. It was a one-room worker's hovel. Its residents, worn down by the entropy of life, moved through its hallways like apparitions. These were the taxi drivers and bargirls. The *Ka Yai,* or Thai mafia footmen, guarded its halls against police raids. When Bangkok gave up on you, this is where you landed. The room he rented had a history. The previous occupant had murdered his wife in the bathroom. The landlady told him this because she was sick of the Thai tenants finding out, and then leaving as soon as they heard the *Phii* crying late at night. Esmeralda didn't mind the ghosts. He had his own entourage from the other side that gazed at him from the foot of his bed each evening – staring at him with their blackened eyeballs and bloated heads, with that *why me?* expression on their faces.

Esmeralda turned off the CD player and geared up for the job. He left on the lingerie just to feel more confident. He walked outside into the furnace blast of the Bangkok sun and looked around. The toupee was already doing its job. He could see the parasites swimming under the skin of passersby. The toupee tinged the world an orchid red, and then he began to see them. It was another one of the side effects, he was told. The temporal lobe epilepsy brought with it a rain of shadows and visions of what some may even call god.

He was already sweating from the jacket and duffel bag full of guns. A shotgun was a bad choice for this gig. He wanted something small and inconspicuous – something feminine like Laura Croft would use. For Esmeralda, Thailand had lost its charm. All of the exotic foods, floral smells, and opium den mystique of the Orient were gone –replaced by the clamor of two-stroke motors and air reeking of diesel smoke and fish sauce. It was just another place on the map where he would draw people's blood. From Sierra Leone to Chechnya, Esmeralda had plied his trade and made money from it. He brought back parasitic souvenirs from four continents and cultivated them within his body. Much of his life was mere bits of fragmented memories. His thoughts turned to the Chinese Guoanbu officer who sculpted children's toys out of Semtex. While making small talk, Esmeralda told him about Bohumil Sole, the scientist who invented Semtex and later strapped some to his body and blew himself up at a bathhouse in the Czech Republic. The irony escaped him, but the Guoanbu officer gave Esmeralda a Semtex panda bear as a souvenir. It was made from a batch that was free of the ethylene glycol dinitrate detection taggant. He told Esmeralda that the panda had a shelf life of twenty years. He also told him that it was enough Semtex to blow up a commercial airliner.

Esmeralda hailed a taxi and hit the ever-present Bangkok traffic within minutes. He looked at his watch. Plenty of time. Little of which he spent reflecting on his past. He gazed out the window of the taxi, as it passed a large group of political protesters. They were taking the stupid route now – decking themselves out in Che Guevara shirts and Chinese red star hats. *That's going to help their cause,* he thought. While you're at it, just get labeled as commies and the Americans will want to see you crushed for sure. He understood the plight of the hapless farmers, though. The entire infrastructure in Thailand was going into making Bangkok the next Hong Kong, while the farmers still lived in shacks. The poor daughters of Isaan went to work in factories or sold their bodies at the bars. It was social Darwinism, just as it was in every other developing country he had visited. The anger on both sides this time was something they couldn't restrain. They, too, were carriers. It was inside all of them. In a short time, the eggs would hatch and everybody would be as one.

He had the taxi pull up at a gas station. He limped as the pain of the emerging Guinea worm shot a jolt through his thigh. He went inside and bought ten gallons of gasoline. He knew from experience that it takes five gallons or more to incinerate a body. If the mark had bodyguards, it still might not be enough. No one knew who had ordered this vendetta. Esmeralda got all of his gigs through a handler, a tactic that kept everybody compartmentalized and safe. It was best to never let the left hand know what the right hand is doing.

As the taxi drove on, Esmeralda put his hand out the window and let the wind flow through his fingers. It felt as though he was running them through a beautiful woman's dirty hair, the hair of a bargirl that chain-smokes. He watched the world through its or-

9

chid tinted lens, sat back, and enjoyed the show. Creatures from some dark and cold part of the universe, with no need for eyes, appeared in the reflections of store windows. As the taxi went by, they reached out for him, seemingly desperate for his company or the warmth of his flesh. He saw past acquaintances in life, and the souls of all those he had killed. His boyhood cat Mr. Noodles sat on top of a car licking his paws. It purred at him as he went by and filled him with the memory of what was perhaps the only creature he had ever loved.

The taxi pulled up to Ekamai bus station. Esmeralda stumbled out with the gas cans and duffel bag, and waved away the various men offering to be his Sherpa.

His text message sounded again.

Walk South 2 blocks. Food stall on corner. Order Kai Giao. Wait.

Esmeralda approached the food stall. The vendor was a hardened, dark-skinned Isaan man. He saw Esmeralda coming and stood open-mouthed in disbelief at the spectacle before him. Esmeralda didn't have to say a word. The food vendor handed him an envelope and told him to sit down.

By now, the sun was directly overhead. It was *tian wan,* as they say in Thai. The sweat dripped down Esmeralda's nose and carried with it the residue of the makeup he had applied. He opened the envelope and pulled out a picture. It wasn't some corporate CEO or head of state. It was a forty-something Farang, along with a beautiful blonde woman. He stared at the picture; enchanted by the woman's features. The delicate curve of her chin, the tiny nose, and perfect spacing of the eyes. It all fell into Pythagoras's Golden Ratio of 0.618, the ratio of perfection in art and nature. The Greek Parthenon had it. Roses had it. Now this girl in the photo. She was close enough in appearance to the celebrity he had always admired. Esmeralda couldn't imagine why anyone would want something so rare and lovely wiped out of existence. He thought about cutting off her face and taking it to a doctor for a transplant. He had read about a woman who had undergone the world's first facial transplant – a successful operation. Perhaps he could cut off her face and put it on ice before he burned her body. Then he could look in the mirror, and, for once, see the Golden Ratio in his own reflection.

****

Esmeralda sat at the edge of the Chao Phraya River, gazing across the water as the sun went down. The bodies were in the trunk. The news reports would later mention a running gun battle, and then an explosion at the convention center. Ostensibly, it was a medical conference. The woman whose face he wanted to wear, put up a fight. He could see them swimming in her eyes as well. Esmeralda would escort them to meet Yama, the lord of the dead. According to Buddhist scripture, it takes four hours and forty minutes for the soul to reach Yama. Wherein Yama would place all of your sins and merit on a scale. He would then determine your rebirth or the realm of hell where you deserved to be tortured The monks recommend not cremating a body before that time has elapsed. There was enough Semtex in the room to incinerate them all. Poor Yama would just have to wait.

He breathed in everything around him. He was drowning in things he could not see. Esmeralda had been born behind a caul – the amniotic sac that clung to a newborn's face at birth. The superstition surrounding it was that a caul-bearer would be a great man or leader, or, as he hoped, a famous blonde celebrity. There were more and more of them now. Businessmen and street food vendors. Taxi drivers and massage girls. Pretty soon, all of them would have it. They would emerge from their cysts and begin with their plans. This job was not bereft of meaning, for the flood would soon come and nothing would hold them back, and then nature would begin the winnowing.

The Chao Phraya River winds into the ocean like a tract of intestine. Only the Hudson and the Ganges rival it in filth. Half of Bangkok's murder weapons are given their final resting place on its floor. Esmeralda chose a place on the Rama VII Bridge and looked around. He pulled out the flaying knife and unwrapped it from the newspaper he kept around it. In the moonlight, the caked blood appeared dark brown. The knife fell from his hands and tumbled towards the water like a lost child returning home. The river welcomed it without ceremony. He thought of following it down there and getting tangled in the hair of the Phii Phrai – the demon ghost of the water that dragged so many Thai people to their deaths. She emitted a light that attracted people into her depths, only to be pulled under to serve as her slaves. His corpse would lay submerged until the gases inside of his body caused it to float. He imagined his corpse, picked free of his lips and eyeballs, floating downstream and out to the ocean, until the waves carried his rotted tongue into the lap of some freshly oiled sunbather on a distant beach.

The worms had their own tactics. Their methodology of warfare was not the destruction of the other side. It was to make the other side do their bidding. To make the other side into their bitch. Shadows, demons, or whatever you choose to call them, remain unseen, yet are all around us. Their eggs have already infected us. The invasion force is already here. They lay dormant within the brain of every creature on the planet. Their goal was not to kill, but to enslave. Esmeralda, the king of parasites. He would be their messiah. He brokered their deals and arranged their coup. He had convinced me of their power. The parasites had evolved. They had intelligence, along with a message to the world. They would begin the next stage of evolution – and our world would become theirs.

The toupee left Esmeralda experiencing Jamais Vu. Ordinary objects seemed alien to him. Looking at his own hand or reflection filled him with dread. The self was an illusion, and the parasites were eating away what was left of his identity. Eventually, he knew, they would strip him of everything – an enviable side effect the Buddhists would hold dear. First you see the beyond. Then you lose your mind. Esmeralda didn't yet know the final stage. But he assumed it was nothing nice.

Part I

The bus ride from Sisaket to Bangkok was eight hours long. I had been scolded by the driver for using the bus's toilet and for spraying the inside of the restroom with a dysenteric jet of shit. My girlfriend Nok came to my defense, sayin I was a fat and stupid farang, and couldn't read the sign in Thai that read "Out of Order."

The noise on the bus left me unable to sleep. Karaoke superstars tormented me with a maddening form of Thai polka. Other passengers wore surgical masks, presumably to keep something out. Babies cried up and down the aisle, and it seemed that every grandma onboard was armed with a toddler. The old women with apathetic eyes and no energy for parenting let the children wail without consolation. They were simply over it. The parents were most likely working in Bangkok – leaving grandma to look after their progeny.

At the rest stop, it was quiet. There were not many travelers this time of night. Nok and I bought rancid *gai ping*, or chicken on a stick, that was cold and fatty. I bought several bags of curry, basil, and shrimp-flavored potato chips while Nok gave me the eye.

"Why you buy so many kanom? Chip make you fat more," she said.

"Because I'm hungry."

"I buy you chicken already. You eat too much."

"That chicken sucked. I don't want to get Salmonella."

"Arai na?" she asked, meaning *what* in Thai.

"Nothing. Mai mii arai."

My usual sentence structure when talking to Nok was inspired by Tarzan, and various caveman movies. It was a mix of English, Thai, and the dialect of the countryside known as Isaan.

"What you say before?"

I sigh deeply, knowing tthis may take a while. "Salmonella."

"What that?"

I revert back to Tarzan mode.

"Something you eat make you sick. Bad thing in food no good."

"No! Chicken okay. I eat many time. No get sick."

"I already sick. Me sick already. I think from chicken we eat before."

I open my fanny pack and pop some Imodium. I have often been told that fanny packs are gay, but it's where I keep my passport and other essentials. I wash the Imodium down with a bottle of honey-lemon green tea, which was another small pleasure of Thailand. Nok's facial expressions ranged from mercurial infant to happy monkey. The one she was showing now said – *what the fuck am I doing with this guy?*

The door to the bus opened, signaling that the driver wanted to leave. These stops, apparently, were for him and not the passengers. As I passed the driver, I could tell he was tweaking. It was not uncommon for the long-haul drivers to smoke ice, or pop yaa baa. The driver confirmed my suspicions when he peeled out of the rest stop and hauled ass along the highway towards Kreungthep.

It had been three months since we were last in Bangkok together. My job as an English teacher had dried up, leaving me unable afford our apartment. The decision was made to move back to Nok's home in the countryside while I called around for work. It had been three months of swatting mosquitoes, shitting in a hole, cooking on a dirt floor, and waking up at five in the morning to the squawk of roosters. I missed my ghetto apartment in Hwai Kwang. I missed my ladyboy neighbors who cranked every Broadway musical known to man. I missed the cries of battered wives, and the howls of feral dogs. In the countryside, I was rotting from the inside. The only thing I could compare it to was being marooned on an island of poorly made shacks, surrounded by an ocean of water buffalo shit.

The news reports were then coming in about another clash with Cambodian troops. The soldiers on both sides adorned their bodies with sak yant tattoos, and carried amulets for protection against the other side's black magic. Nok's home had a bomb shelter in the backyard made from cement and sandbags. At night, we could hear the 105-millimeter rounds exploding in the distance. They gradually got closer as the artillery was walked up. The decision was made to leave again. Her family would stay with relatives farther inland. Nok and I would head back to Bangkok, with the expectation that I would find a job to support everyone. No pressure whatsoever.

The karaoke torture continued all the way to Mochit bus station in Bangkok. I chatted briefly with a couple of Mormon missionaries. They stopped talking to me when I asked them if they were going to work for the CIA when they were done. Apparently the alphabet agencies liked to recruit Mormons because they were square and had experience living overseas. I'd lived overseas for years, but nobody had approached me to become a spook, which made me feel slighted.

The Mochit terminal was huge. Hundreds of people lay strewn around like corpses on the floor as they waited for their departures. Nok led me through the clusterfuck of travelers to the taxi stand.

She spat out a machinegun riff in the Isaan dialect and the driver agreed to take us where she asked. Inside the taxi, Nok showed me a modicum of affection. She put her legs across mine and used me as a footstool. This, it seemed, was the gist of our relationship. The motion of the taxi made her fall asleep within minutes. I looked at the brown skin on her legs and the delicate curve of her cheeks. The gods balanced out her beauty by giving her one of the crankiest dispositions known to man.

I looked out the window as the cab made its way to the Bang Kapi area of Bangkok. Various cars that passed by had stuffed animals hanging from the rear bumper. I had asked Nok about this phenomenon, and she told me it was to prevent ghosts from causing traffic accidents. She informed me that the accidents were not caused by people driving recklessly, but by the angry spirits of those who had died a premature death. In Bangkok, I rarely saw a child with a toy or stuffed animal. The former were used as offerings to the ghosts that bar girls prayed to, and the later as a talisman for bad drivers.

Our cab passed through several police checkpoints. This was how the cops busted yaa baa dealers. People on scooters or in taxis transported most drugs that moved through the city. The nightly news ran ongoing stories of shootouts with the police. In a country where trafficking could get you the death penalty, many drug dealers opted for taking their chances with a pistol instead of a judge. At the third checkpoint, the cops stopped our car.

I willed Nok to wake up with the power of my mind – to no avail. The kind and fair officer asked to see my luggage. Sure, no problem. The taxi driver popped the trunk and the officer opened my suitcase. Nearly all the taxis in Bangkok were Toyota Corollas, which ran on natural gas. Half of the trunk space was taken up by a large fuel tank, leaving very little room for a suitcase, let alone moving a body. I often wondered how I would dispose of Nok's remains after I killed her during one of our fights. Our future together seemed written in the stars.

The officer found no illicit drugs in my bag. But I was just as nervous that he might find some that had magically appeared and required the payment of an on-the-spot fine. I was low on cash and worried I wouldn't have enough to pay a fine if the officer decided to impose one.

The officer handed me my passport, and I was free to go. Several military Humvees rolled by with gunners manning the fifty cal on top. This was not an uncommon sight. There were always protests with the different colored shirt people. Oftentimes, shit just popped off and the whole city was under martial law. The Thai Army used America's hand-me-downs. Troops could be seen driving in Vietnam-era M-60 tanks and carrying M-79 grenade launchers – guns I recognized from playing too many video games.

By the time we reached our hotel off of Lad Prao 150, it had been a ten-hour journey. I liked this neighborhood because it had fewer foreigners than the touristy areas. The only farangs I saw were the ones who trained at the local Muay Thai gym. I had trained there when I was younger and had delusions of becoming a pro fighter. Injury after injury led me to the conclusion that I was better off fat and letting people kick my ass.

I had come to Thailand because I could no longer afford to live in Los Angeles. New geography changed nothing in my life. It followed me wherever I ran. Back home, I was even more of a fuck up. I had bad credit and a studio apartment. I shopped for food and just about everything else at the 99 Cent Store. My fatness could be attributed to a diet of Taco Bell dollar burritos and gas station hot dogs. All of that changed when I first came to Thailand. For a few dollars a day, I could eat like a king. I had an apartment with cable and Internet for less than two hundred bucks a month.

Like so many men, I had fallen in love with the beauty of Thai women. Even the poorest have their hierarchy, and to Nok I was slightly less of a deadbeat than my Thai male counterparts. Nothing beat going out with a beautiful girl with low standards. Nok had grown up in a shack on stilts near the Cambodian border. It was a primitive existence bordering on post-apocalyptic survival. The way mankind had lived for thousands of years before we became a bunch of spoiled pussies with steel appliances and granite countertops. Living with her in the countryside reminded me of how soft I had truly become.

We checked into the hotel and hauled our own stuff up to the room. There were no bellhops in the three hundred Baht per night dives we slept in. Our only vices were hot water and air conditioning. If the hotel had a Western toilet, we felt as if we had won the lottery.

We took hot showers to remove the grime of traveling cross-country. I had to wash myself three times just to get the stench off. I lay in bed for the first time in months – in Sisaket, we had slept on the floor. I watched as Nok walked around the room naked. She reminded me of the seventies film star Laura Gemser. *Emmanuelle in Bangkok* was a movie that had deeply affected my childhood psyche. For years, I must have carried her image in my subconscious mind until I met Nok at the restaurant where she worked. Now she strolled around the room, secure in her beauty. We had been together for two years, and I never got tired of looking at her.

Nok climbed into bed. She put her arms around me to give what I thought was a hug. Instead, she was simply looking for the TV remote under my pillow. Nok flipped the channels on the tube, and I cringed at what I knew was coming. It would be another three hours of Thai soap operas or variety shows. Sometimes it was enough to make me want to put a gun in my mouth.

I stared at the ceiling and watched a jing jok lizard sullenly munching on an insect.

"Honey, what that?" Nok asked.

"What's what?"

"Doo tii wii!" she commanded.

I sat up and looked at the television. The screen showed a riot taking place near Siam Paragon mall. There were lines of police with riot shields forming a phalanx. I didn't see any masses of red or yellow shirts indicating a political rally.

"I dunno, babe."

The voice of the reporter sounded frantic.

"Lady she say every people go crazy."

"Cool, maybe the world's coming to an end."

I lay my head back on the pillow. My lizard friend was now gone.

"Oi! Lady she say maybe people they take too much yaa baa."

"Yaa baa's a helluva drug," I sighed.

Nok's attention span was that of a fly. She changed the channel to the familiar sounds of crying women with cheating husbands. I turned my head to see Nok with her eyes fixed on the TV. I reached out to stroke her skin, but my affection was rebuffed. The honeymoon phase was officially over. I fell asleep thinking of how I would dispose of her body.

****

I awoke to the peaceful sound of Nok breathing. Gone were the annoyances of my home country. I used to fantasize about shooting the leaf blower guy who spent two hours a day in my apartment complex deliberately trying to piss me off. I had wanted to kill many people in Los Angeles, for no particular reason other than that they had irritated me. LA brought out the worst in people. It brought out the worst in me. All big cities had this effect. From Chicago to San Francisco, I felt the walls closing in. I had even tried moving to Hawaii, but the claustrophobic realization that I was trapped on a rock in the middle of the Pacific Ocean made me leave after three weeks.

I never grew tired of Bangkok. I knew people who flew directly to Phuket and avoided the City of Angels like a plague. In Bangkok, only your imagination and your wallet limited you. Anything was possible. If getting dressed up in lingerie and choked to death by ladyboys was your thing, you were in good company.

I walked to the balcony to smoke a cigarette. I chose L&Ms because they were cheap and had a delightful picture of a dying cancer patient on the package to serve as a warning. When I opened the curtains, the cigarette fell from my lips. In the distance, I could see plumes of smoke coming from the area I'd seen on the news. Siam Paragon was where the wealthy shopped for Louis Vuitton and other accoutrements of douchebaggery. I had lived here during the violent street protests, when life had gone on in the city beyond the immediate area of chaos. I looked down at the street below. Traffic was backed up even on the side sois.

Part of me hoped for a zombie outbreak. If that happened, I knew exactly where I would go. I had daydreamed the apocalypse so many times. I pictured myself looting a pharmacy and taking all of the painkillers and antibiotics. In the aftermath of whatever shitstorm engulfed the world, I could barter my sack of drugs for anything I needed.

I longed for nature to start over – the same thing that appealed to everyone from Christians who prayed for the rapture to the man who joined the French Foreign Legion. It was the opportunity to be born again, to be forgiven the mistakes of your current life, allowing you to remake yourself and your history. A swarm of flesh-eating corpses would be just what this city needed for society to begin again and let nature choose its new leaders.

I turned on the news and every channel blasted the coverage. People were going apeshit. The area surrounding Siam Paragon was pure bedlam. A news cameraman caught an image of a Humvee gunner turning his .50 cal on his fellow soldiers and wasting them. Two M-60 tanks aimed their guns at each other and blew each other to shit. Cops were no longer in a phalanx. They were beating the fuck out of and shooting other cops – or just about anyone else that happened to be around them. It seemed like a wave of mass insanity – exactly what I'd pictured the end of the world to look like.

I changed the channel. The other news station showed footage of a group of toddlers at the zoo. They were biting each other – digging their teeth down to the bone. The parents got in on the deal and picked up their children to use as weapons against other parents. The footage ended with the cameraman swinging his camera at one parent's head – knocking out an eyeball – before someone tackling him to the ground. The camera fell at an angle that showed tigers in a cage. The striped felines seemed aloof and unaffected by whatever was going on. I figured it was because the tigers at the Thai zoos were fucked up on tranquilizers.

I nudged Nok to wake up. She opened her eyes slowly and scrunched up her face. It was like watching the hatching of a sea turtle.

"Nok, something's happening. I need you to translate."

I turned up the volume on the TV. Nok sat up, but held her head down, listening.

"Why you wake me up? Stupid fat farang! TV only say that people fighting! People always fighting in Thailand. You wake me up again and I going to cut off your gluay kaeng!"

Nok flopped back on the bed and was asleep immediately.

My blood was starting to boil. Everything I had done for this little shit, and this is how she treats me? I took several deep breaths, but my heart and mind were racing as if I were hopped up on a mixture of meth and schizophrenia. I heard a voice in my head saying *do it.*

My mind was flooded with thoughts on how to kill her. My hands reached out for her throat, but it was replaced by another thought urging me to stab her in the eyes and cut out her tongue. I stood up and spun around in circles looking for anything sharp. I saw the images on the television, then saw myself in the mirror. I was acting the same as the people on TV. My hands shook as I dived for my suitcase. I ripped through my medicine bag and retrieved my bottle of Xanax. I chewed an entire two-milligram bar and let it dissolve sublingually. Just for good measure, I crushed another Xannie bar and snorted it.

I sat down on the floor and listened. I could hear my heartbeat in my ears. Veins protruded from my face and throbbed in my temples. It felt as though explosions were happening behind my eyes. I looked up at Nok. The violent impulses were subsiding as the Xanax calmed me down. In the rooms next door, I could hear banging against the walls, followed by screaming from both men and women. A foot kicked at my door…and again…louder now, as though a SWAT team were trying to enter. There was a scream and a scuffle outside my door. I heard the twang of metal hitting bone, and then footsteps running down the hall accompanied by the maniacal laughter of the insane or possessed.

I looked up at the TV. One of the news anchors was sticking a pen into the neck of her co-host. Then the screen went blank.

Whatever it was – it was airborne. My mind raced to cover the possibilities. My top picks were terrorist attack, water supply tampering, alien toxic mold, demonic possession, mass hysteria, or a virus.

I turned my head. Nok was kicking in her sleep as though locked in a nightmare. I grabbed a couple of Xanax and tiptoed toward her. I'd have to do this quick. If she woke up and started fighting, I knew I could overpower her, but she might get lucky and take out an eye.

My plan was to sit on her and shove the pills down her throat. My mind flashed back to the times I had tried to wrestle with my Rottweiler to make her take her vitamins – followed by her spitting them out or trying to bite me. My thinking was clear. Two Xanax bars usually knocked me on my ass. Now it seemed as if their effect was only to counteract my violent impulses. In one quick move, I shoved the pills in her mouth and gave her a quick donkey punch to the kidneys to make her swallow them.

Nok jumped up and ran to the bathroom.

After apologizing for hurting her – and saying, "I love you" – I explained what I'd seen on the news. I offered my theories regarding the cause, but gave up when the Tarzan vocabulary prohibited me from explaining demonic possession or terrorist attacks.

"Give me my clothes," she whispered through the door.

I gathered up her stuff, and handed it to her when she cracked the door. I had no desire to force it open and yell at her. The Xannie did what it was designed for: Make someone not give a shit.

I spent the better part of an hour trying to coax Nok out of the bathroom. In the distance, I heard the din of gunshots and car crashes, screams, and the sounds of dying. I tried to bait her out with the promise of papaya salad. When that didn't work, I pledged the purchase of a gold bracelet. When she finally came out, she was skittish. Her previous boyfriend was an Aussie who used to beat her. I remembered our pillow talk one night when in a sad, quiet voice, she asked me if I would ever do the same. I promised her I wouldn't, and told her I'd never raised my hand to a woman. But now her defenses were up. I had to do damage control and figure out what had happened.

I went to the door and listened. Everything was quiet. I worked up the balls to open the door and look into the hallway. There was no body lying on the floor, but there was a huge amount of blood and arterial spray on the walls. I was actually relieved to see the blood. The red splotches and spatter made the whole experience real – without the evidence, I would have thought I'd imagined the entire episode and was losing my mind. Nok peeked over my shoulder and let out a gasp. I closed the door and locked it with the chain, then propped one of the chairs against the door for good measure.

The balcony was the only other exit to the room. I walked over to it and looked outside. The fires still burned, and blood covered the streets and cars. The coppery stench rose up in the heat of the day, and I could smell it three floors up. Nok turned on the TV. She switched stations and each played the Thai national anthem, indication that the channel was off the air.

I opened the minibar and grabbed a beer. How long had we slept? This much carnage could not have unfolded overnight. Nok tried her cell phone and called her mom. After a long delay, her mother answered. Nok spoke too fast for me to understand any of it. But I could read the tears in her eyes and could hear her mother screaming into the phone with rage. Nok threw the phone on the ground and collapsed into my arms.

"Is your mom okay?" I asked, already knowing the answer.

Nok could barely get the words out.

"I ask how my sister is and my little cousin. My mom she say she kill them already when they sleeping and she say she want me to come home so she can kill me, too."

****

We had enough food in the minibar to last a couple of days. We were both too afraid to leave the room. Even if we did, we didn't know where to go. I had to assume that the violence was citywide, perhaps even countrywide since it had affected Nok's village. I counted out my Xanax. I had thirty-two doses left from a prescription for sixty. I had told my doctor that I was afraid of flying. In truth, I was a pill head. I could stay in bed all day on a mixture of bliss and apathy, just letting the chemicals cradle my brain and soothe my soul. Xannie had a short half-life. If this thing were still spreading, Nok and I would need to take three or four doses a day. I had no idea why a benzodiazepine would work against this thing, but it did, and that's all I cared about.

"We can't stay here," I said.

Nok stared at the wall and didn't answer.

"Nok, do you want to stay here while I go downstairs?"

Nothing.

"I'm gonna go check out the lobby and see if this thing is over with, okay?"

Nok nodded.

I opened the door to the room and stepped into the hall, careful not to make any noise. I looked both ways – it was all clear except for the blood. I walked towards the stairway and past the other rooms. The doors were wide open and blood covered everything. I couldn't see any bodies. Cheap paintings of naked Asian women in a river bathing scene adorned the walls. Blood spatter freckled the painting, transforming the work to a depiction of Cambodia's killing fields. I looked down the staircase and listened. Nothing but the slow drip of blood as it fell from the railings. My heart pounded in my throat as I made my way down several flights to the lobby.

It was the same scene as I'd witnessed everywhere else in the hotel. Blood covered the walls and floor from arterial spray. I believed, and perhaps this was delusional, that my years of watching *Forensic Files* and reading true crime novels qualified me to interpret the evidence These were kill shots. Whoever did the slashing was going for the throat or vital organs. The adage about killing came to mind: "Stop the breathing, start the bleeding, and induce shock." The thought made me wonder if that was common knowledge, or if I was just a psychopath.

I looked through the double glass doors onto the street. A small person – possibly a kid – darted past the entrance in a full sprint. A few beats later, a kid wielding a machete ran after him. I glued myself to the side of the doorway and inched my way onto the street. I looked to my right and saw the kids a block away. The first kid now had a rifle in his hand. An Army Humvee stood next to the child – probably where he'd obtained an abandoned weapon. The kid with the rifle leveled it at the other boy and fired. Puffs of pink mist erupted from the machete carrier's body as he fell to the ground. The boy with the gun looked down the street, spotted me, and took off running again.

That was another good sign. If everybody was killing each other, this boy should have killed me, too. The fact that he didn't meant not everyone was affected. I looked up. Even the trees had blood high up in the branches. I assumed that the birds took part in the slaughter as well. I saw the Humvee where the boy had found gun and decided to try my luck. I sprinted towards it and paused as I approached the machete boy lying in the street. There was a small entrance wound in the front and a larger one in the back. I stepped over him and looked inside the Humvee, where I found a hand grenade but no guns.

I pocketed the hand grenade and turned towards the hotel. The machete boy appeared asleep. Other than the bullet hole in his chest, he seemed to be in a state of catatonia – but not dead. His eyes were open, and I looked into them for any sign of life. I saw something move in the whites of his eyes. It was small, like a worm or a leech. I saw movement under the boy's skin as though something were crawling beneath the surface. I didn't hang around to find out what.

I hightailed it back to the hotel and knocked on the door. Nok didn't answer,

"It's me. Open the door, honey."

Nothing. I knocked again.

"Babe, open up."

I felt my stomach turn and my legs get weak as my mind prepared for the worst. I stepped back to kick in the door when Nok finally opened up.

"Why you leave me?"

I pushed her inside the room and closed the door.

"What you have in your pocket?" she asked.

I pulled out the grenade and showed her.

"What you see outside?"

"Lots of blood, but only a few bodies."

"Maybe they go to hospital?"

"I don't think so."

"So what we do?"

"I don't know."

I sat on the bed and thought about our dilemma. I didn't know what was on the streets beyond this area. Until we had some kind of plan, I didn't want to take any chances. I got up and walked to the door.

"Where you go? Don't leave me again."

"I'm just going to get us some food. I'll be back in a few minutes."

I shut the door on Nok, just as she was beginning to complain. I walked into each of the rooms on our floor and opened the minibars. I took a couple of pillowcases and filled them full of chocolate bars, potato chips, water and beer, then went back to our room and locked the door.

****

I was low on cigarettes and considered going outside to find a shop I could loot. I smoked the last of my pack on the balcony as I looked down to the street. A lone man, dressed in a suit and tie, staggered between the cars. I could tell he was a farang, maybe a Latino, and he appeared in his mid twenties. He carried a large, hard-shelled suitcase and seemed drunk. Before I could duck back into the room, he looked up at me. First he stopped walking, and then he stared at me.

"Hey buddy, you got a cigarette?" I yelled down to him.

The man looked around, and then looked back up to me.

"What the fuck is going on here, man?" he yelled back. He was American.

"Some crazy shit. You got any smokes?"

The man patted his suit pocket and pulled out a pack. He opened them and looked inside.

"Yeah man, I got like…five left. I got a carton in my bag. You need one?"

"That would be tits," I yelled back.

"Huh?"

"Tits!"

"Oh…yeah," he said. It seemed as though his brain was a few seconds behind.

The man looked down the street, up at the sky, down to his feet, and over his shoulder, then back at me. "Well…you coming down to get 'em?"

"Can you just like, leave them on top of one of the cars or something?"

The man looked at the car next to him. His head wobbled. Definitely drunk.

"Quit being a pussy and come down. I ain't gonna bite," he yelled. He did seem rather nonthreatening.

"Okay, bro, I'll be down in a sec."

The man nodded and gave me the thumbs up. He looked to his left and let out a yelp. "Oh fuck! Open the door! Don't come down!"

The man tried braking into a sprint and then fell on his face. He popped back up, lifted the suitcase over his head, and hauled ass to the hotel entrance. I looked at Nok.

"Hide in the bathroom!" I told her.

"Arai na?"

"Go in bathroom. Bpai hong naam!" I said and bolted out the door. I jumped stairs three at a time and made it down to the lobby.

The man banged on the double glass doors so hard I was surprised they didn't shatter.

"Open the fucking door!" he screamed.

I raced up to the door and undid the latch. He jumped inside the lobby, spun around, and helped me close the doors.

"We gotta go, where's your room?"

"On the first floor. Room 223," I said.

There was no way I was letting him up on the third floor with Nok. If this were the end of the world, Nok would be in demand to repopulate the Earth – that, or serving as a slave to mutant biker gangs. It had only been the apocalypse for three weeks, and I wasn't sure if survivors were in rape mode yet.

The man bounded up the stairs to the first floor and took off down the hall. I waited in the lobby, hiding behind a paper cutout of a Thai Airways stewardess making a *wai* with her hands. I wanted to see what the man saw. If it was a group of killers on a rampage, or a seven-year-old kid with a chainsaw, I wanted to know what I was up against.

I waited…nothing came.

I ran up the stairs after the dude. Halfway down the hall, I checked myself for a weapon. I only had the grenade and a pen in my pocket. I palmed the pen prison-shank style and went into room 223.

The dude was there. He had his suitcase open on the bed. Inside was brick after brick of white, powdery substances wrapped in plastic. The dude cut open a bag and buried his nose in it Scarface style.

"Shit, is that coke?" I asked.

The man snorted in a small mountain, then collapsed on the floor.

"Chi-naaaa…"

I was impressed. I had never seen so much heroin in one place. It was like walking around with a death sentence in your bag.

"Where'd you get that?" I asked him, not thinking.

The dude sat on the floor. All of his facial muscles were relaxed, and his eyelids made him look like a tired dog.

"Airport, bro. I was getting ready to go through customs when it went down."

"How did you get out?"

"Probably did the same as you. You locked yourself inside, right? I hid in a bathroom, and listened while people were screaming outside. I saw people getting torn apart and stomping their babies' heads. It was as war zone – only there were no sides. Everybody killed everybody."

I took in more of his image. Prison tattoos peeked out from the sleeves of his suit. His head was shaved, but growing out, and he rocked a pencil-thin mustache and soul patch.

"Why weren't you affected?"

The dude spoke slowly. "I don't know, man. I was pretty fucked up on Valium and booze when I went through customs. I saw a few other people at the airport that weren't affected, either. They just got butchered and eaten by the ones that went nuts."

"Where you heading to?"

"I was trying to make in to Pattaya. I heard that all of Walking Street is getting defended. The survivors turned every beer bar and go-go club into a mini-fortress. Kind of like in that movie with the chick with the big titties. There are a shitload of British and American Marines and sailors on shore leave, and they're trying to repel the mass assaults of the afflicted."

I put my hand out. "I'm Joel."

"They call me Vato," he said, shaking my hand.

"You have a plan to get to Pattaya?"

"Did it look like I had a plan when you saw me? I stole a taxi, and then a Tuk-tuk. I would have taken a scooter if I didn't have this big-ass suitcase with me. There are cars everywhere with the keys still inside. Transportation isn't a problem as long as you don't mind running into a horde."

"What did you see outside when you came running in?"

"You didn't see them yet?"

"See what?"

"Hang on," Vato said and stuck his face back into the pile of heroin. He must have done enough to kill Nikki Sixx. "The monkeys…you didn't see the monkeys yet?"

"What monkeys?" I asked.

"Damn, homie, you been living in this room with no TV? You haven't been outside yet? Check it out. The monkeys…let's see, how do I put it? The monkeys are dead, but they ain't really dead."

"You've seen them?"

"Yeah, man, they're fucking psychotic. They just swing off the trees and power lines and rip your face off. I saw a dude with a gun trying to shoot one. He missed every shot. They're fast as fuck, and they don't stop for shit."

Vato debriefed me on the state of affairs in Thailand. There had been a total media blackout. No Internet, no cell phones, no television or radio. He told me that after people were attacked, they went into a deep sleep but didn't die. When they woke up, they turned into cannibalistic psychopaths. They became the afflicted. The ones I saw on the news. The ones in my hotel. Before I popped the Xanax, I was almost one myself. This led me to my theory, which I shared with Vato.

"This thing must already be inside of us. You and I are carriers. The only thing holding it at bay is the drugs we're on."

"Yeah, no shit," he said.

"This thing can also be transmitted through a bite, right?"

"As far as I can tell, yes."

"Who at the airport didn't become afflicted?"

"I saw people in the airport bars putting up a fight."

"Right. They were drinking, I was on Xannie, and you were on a bunch of different shit. You see?"

Vato looked at me as if I were retarded. As if this great epiphany wasn't clear and apparent.

"Yeah, man, I know already. The only ones who didn't go nuts were the ones getting fucked up. That's why Pattaya held out, because there are so many drunks in that town. There are probably pockets of survivors in Patpong, Nana, Soi Cowboy, and every other part of this country where people get hammered."

"So why go all the way to Pattaya? Why not just go to Soi Cowboy or Nana Plaza? There's sure to be drunks there," I said.

"I'm not going to Pattaya for the drunks. I gotta deliver this fucking bag of China or I'm dead. I gotta give it back to the Ka Yai since I couldn't get it on a plane. I talked to one of them before the phones went dead. He said bring it to Pattaya."

The Ka Yai was the Thai mafia. The name meant "Big Leg." As scary as they were, I thought Vato's logic was flawed.

"What's the point? You'll probably die just trying to get there. They'll probably die soon, too. I think you just inherited a big-ass bag of China for free, man."

Vato nodded his head as he pondered this.

"Yeah, man. I think you're right. Extenuating circumstances huh?"

"I think end of the world qualifies, yes."

"All right, man, sounds good. High Five!"

He high-fived me.

"Porno handshake," I said, extending a bent elbow to him.

"Porno handshake?"

"You bump elbows. Like, because you got dirty hands after making a porno, get it?"

Vato extended an elbow to me, and we bumped.

"I like that one. Gotta remember that. Porno handshake. Porno handshake. Porno handshake. Yeah. I like it," he muttered as if in slow motion. It was creepy.

For a long minute, we sat in an uncomfortable silence, and then I remembered Nok upstairs.

"Shit. I'll be back. Just chill here," I said

"Where you going, homie?"

"I forgot something upstairs."

"I'll go with you, man," Vato said and started to get up.

"No, no, no. It's cool, man. I'll be right back."

"You got a girl upstairs don't you? No wonder you didn't leave the hotel for three weeks. Bring her down bro, and we'll party. I ain't no booty bandit. Don't worry, homie."

I thought about the pen in my pocket. I thought about sticking him in the neck. This was one of my normal violent thoughts. Nothing to signal I was being afflicted.

"Just wait here and I'll be back."

Vato plunged his face into the pile of heroin. I could almost hear his liver crying. I went upstairs to check on Nok. The door to the room was open, and she wasn't in the bathroom. I called out her name. Nothing. I looked down the hallway and ran into each room yelling her name. Still nothing. I looked out the windows and didn't see her. I ran back to our room and went to the balcony.

"Fuck!" I shouted. Bedsheets were tied to the railing, prison-escape style. I wondered how far she could have gone. Then I thought about the monkeys.

I ran back to Vato. "She's gone, we gotta go look for her."

I threw Vato an empty backpack. "Put the China in there. You can't lug that suitcase around. Let's go, man."

Vato didn't move. Maybe he thought I was trying to alpha male him. He was an ex-con, and not used to getting bossed around.

"Homie, sabai sabai. You ain't gonna find her. Either the afflicted got her or the monkeys ate her."

****

The city was nearly empty. I saw flashes in my peripheral vision of figures darting between buildings, and I could feel a presence, stalking us from behind the abandoned cars. Everything that made Bangkok vibrant was gone. The remnants of once-busy markets sat forlorn in the baking sun. We wandered among the detritus of food stalls and bootleg DVD vendors, whose wares still lay as pickings for the ghosts of tourists and as a toilet for the birds who still waged war above. We found a shop with gardener supplies and helped ourselves to a couple of machetes – then walked in an expanding circle around the hotel. I left notes on the windshields of cars and tuk-tuks, telling Nok to wait for us back at the room and hang a sheet from the balcony if she was there.

As we came around the hotel on our third lap, I saw an indistinct figure. I rubbed my eyes and refocused on the image. It was a man. He was wearing a pink dress and carrying an axe over his right shoulder. In his left hand, he carried a large cooler.

Vato and I ducked into the doorway of a pharmacy and whispered to each other. I peered out from behind the wall and tried to spy the man again. His dress was covered in blood and the soft tissue of a recent kill. He walked a few paces and then turned around and looked up at the trees. Then he scanned the ground, as if searching for something. He walked in our direction. The man in the dress was now on our side of the street. There was no way we could hide in the doorway and no way we could walk back on the street without him seeing us. Vato and I decided on an ambush.

We held the machetes in our best Conan poses and prepared ourselves to look threatening. About ten yards from our position in the doorway, I heard the slow shuffle of tired footsteps. It was a decent enfilade for an ambush. A few yards away, the man stopped walking. Vato looked at me, as if asking what should we do.

"Are you two sailors lonely?" the man called out to us, "'Cause I just might be the last woman on Earth if you boys wanna party."

Vato and I just looked at each other. Vato mouthed the words *what the fuck?*

"Come on out, boys. Don't make mama come get you," the man said again. He sounded like Demi Moore.

Vato and I seemed to grow balls at the same time. We jumped out from the doorway with our machetes raised. I even made a feeble war cry. The man was unimpressed. I don't even think he blinked. He stood with the aloof air of a condescending French waiter.

He giggled.

"Wassup bro?" Vato said.

"Have you boys seen my dog? He's a little white puffball," the man said.

His whole image: The dress covered in gore, the axe over his shoulder, and on his head arguably the worst toupee I had ever seen – something along the lines of Donald Trump's hair. Vato and I didn't respond.

"His name is Sparkles. Have you seen him?" the man said again.

"Sorry man, no," said Vato.

"You can relax with those big swords of yours. I won't eat you."

Vato and I lowered our machetes.

"Where you coming from?" I asked the man.

"Just been doing some silly stuff. You boys want to help me find my dog Sparkles?"

"Can't. I'm looking for my wife," I told him.

"Maybe we can look together. What does she look like?"

"Tall blonde with big boobies," I told him.

Vato shot me a look.

"Big ones like mine?" the man asked.

He didn't have big boobies.

"We gotta go. Good luck finding your dog," Vato said.

"You're just going to leave a lady all by herself in this town, with the afflicted, and the monkeys running around?"

"How come you didn't become afflicted? What drugs were you doing?" I asked.

"Drugs? What drugs?"

I thought about another angle. Those that hadn't gone mad had been doing drugs or getting hammered. Perhaps there was another segment of society that was immune to its effects – those that were already insane.

"Never mind," I told him.

"You boys hear about Pattaya?"

Vato and I nodded.

"You boys heading there?'

We nodded again.

"Can a lady tag along? There's strength in numbers. I'm pretty good with this thing as you can see by my dress," the man said and lifted the weight of the axe in his hand as though it was a feather. In response, Vato and I both tightened the grips on our machetes.

"What's your name?" Vato asked.

"I'm Esmeralda."

"I'm Vato, this is Joel."

A scream cut into our obligatory introductions. It echoed down the street and was followed by another. I had heard Nok cry a million times over everything from stubbing her toe to the death of a relative. I had never heard her scream, but I assumed this one was hers.

"That's her, I know it," I said, and took off running.

I expected Vato and Esmeralda to be my backup. They weren't. I looked over my shoulder as I ran, and they stood motionless, watching my suicidal act of heroism. I ran towards the screams and could tell it was coming towards me.

Through the maze of abandoned cars and dumped scooters, I jumped the obstacles and pulled the hand grenade from my pocket. I had thrown a total of four grenades in my life – all of them in Cambodia, for five dollars apiece. The nervous Cambodian had held my hand through the process of pulling the pin and chucking it into a pond to prevent the fragmentation from killing us both. I had been wasted at the time, and now I couldn't remember the cook-off time for the grenade.

I rounded a corner, and the screaming stopped. I saw Nok in the middle of the street. She was down on her knees, placing her head to the ground in respect to the Buddha. I panned my gaze up. A horde of afflicted was fighting with a troupe of monkeys. The monkeys' attacks were savage. They jumped on top of the afflicted's heads and began tearing at their eyeballs. The afflicted, in turn, grabbed the monkeys by their heads and ripped out their throats by the teeth. Nok was bleeding and her arms were covered in bite marks. I knelt beside her and touched her back gently.

"Baby, we gotta go," I whispered, but she didn't respond. I wrapped my arm around her torso and lifted her up. She was a spinner. No more than ninety pounds. As I raised her slight body from the ground, I felt grateful I wasn't a chubby chaser.

The afflicted that weren't fighting with the monkeys turned their attention to us. I threw Nok over my shoulder and pulled the pin on the grenade. No more than a second after I pulled it, I let it fly from my hand. It missed completely and landed behind the horde by about ten yards. I turned and ran as fast as I could with a ninety-pound Thai girl over my shoulder.

When the grenade went off, I had just rounded the corner onto the street where Vato and the tranny were standing. The grenade caught the gas tank of a nearby car and sent up what looked like a fiery geyser.

Esmeralda began traipsing towards me. Vato stood back and evaluated the risks of getting involved in my plight. I looked over my shoulder and the afflicted were swarming on us. As Esmeralda came running past me, I picked up the pace. I spun on my heels to see him raise his axe and bring it down on one of the afflicted's head. Its skull split open down the middle, all the way to the shoulders – leaving the head and neck in two separate halves.

"Go grab that tuk-tuk over there," Esmeralda said. He wasn't panicking. "Hurry, these things are stinky."

Vato beat me to the tuk-tuk and revved it up. I was expecting him to leave us there, but, to his credit, he waited. Nok was sniffling as I held her on my shoulder and put her in the back seat. I put a leg up on the tuk-tuk, still thinking that Vato might take off with my girl to go and repopulate the world.

Esmeralda was in a blood frenzy. He swung his axe as the afflicted closed in around him. Below, the ground grew littered with corpses. I gathered he had done this before.

"Hurry the fuck up!" Vato yelled.

Esmeralda swung the axe one last time, and then jogged over to us.

"Now I'm all sweaty," he said.

"Drive!" I said.

The tuk-tuk had three wheels and motorcycle handles, along with the gearshift of an automobile – not easy to drive unless you did it for a living. Vato worked the clutch and ground the gears until the metal shrieked.

"Fucking piece of shit," he cursed.

The tuk-tuk finally lurched forward in spurts as Vato figured out the shifting. He hit the gas and the tuk-tuk sped away with the whine of its two-stroke motor. It belched out a plume of smoke, like a blood trail for sharks to follow.

We drove on the sidewalks and between the abandoned cars that clogged the streets. I rubbed Nok's head where she was bleeding and looked at the bite marks on her arms.

"From the monkeys?"

She turned her head towards me. Her expression was vacant. Something moved in the whites of her eyes. "How you know about that?"

"The guy driving is named Vato. He told me about them."

"Yes. Many monkey bite me," she said.

"How did you get away from them?"

"Monkey start fighting with people you see come. Oi, what happening?"

I had no answer, and she saw it on my face. We both left it at that. I looked to Esmeralda who sat in front of me.

"Nice work back there. Where should we go?"

Esmeralda held his hand out the side of the tuk-tuk and let the wind hold it aloft. The front of his bad Donald Trump toupee lifted in the draft of the open vehicle.

"We need to get on the elevated tollway and head towards Pattaya," he said, and then leaned forward and spoke to Vato. I couldn't hear what they said through the din of the engine whine. Vato said something back to Esmeralda, and then Esmeralda turned to me.

"Vato knows how to get there. But first we need to make a detour."

I simply wanted to get out of Bangkok – preferably to a beach. If were any boats were still there, I would jack one and get Nok and me someplace safe. In my head, I ran through different scenarios. I pictured the full moon partygoers on Koh Phi Phi getting monumentally fucked up on ecstasy and fighting to remain the last bastion of hippie life on the island. I envisioned gangs of armed ladyboys holding the line on Walking Street, killing the afflicted in between hits from their ice pipes, then going off to service the American and British sailors in town. No apocalypse scenario was complete without armed gangs of bandits raiding the countryside on motorcycles. Since this was Thailand, I substituted badass-looking motorcycles with Hello Kitty scooters and motorized rice plows.

I looked back at Esmeralda, "Where's our detour?"

"We have to go to Siriraj hospital. Across the Chao Phraya River."

"For?"

"I'm getting a surgical procedure."

I tilted my head a little, "Now?"

"Not now. I just need to pick up a surgeon that works there. I know where he is hiding out."

Siriraj hospital was in the other direction. This was a point-less detour and Esmeralda was obviously insane.

"I don't think that's a good idea."

Esmeralda's voice boomed as if broadcast from the demon god Rahu's lungs. "We are going to Siriraj hospital or I will peel your face off and chop up your little brown monkey of a girl-friend!"

I held up my machete and cocked it back to take a swing. There was absolutely no possibility of such a maneuver happen-ing in the back of a speeding tuk-tuk. Esmeralda's demeanor calmed down, and his voice normalized to that of a gruff shemale phone-sex operator.

"I'm sorry. I should explain myself," Esmeralda opened the cooler he carried and pulled out what appeared to be a piece of meat wrapped in plastic. He reached inside and removed the item. Esmeralda turned away, and held the object over his face and made adjustments. When he turned around again, he was wearing the flayed, rotting face of a female. The image was comical and not even remotely terrifying, despite its *Texas Chainsaw Massa-cre* overtones.

"Who am I?" Esmeralda asked.

I chortled, then responded: "Tyra Banks."

The skin of the face was white.

"No. Guess again."

"Sally Struthers?"

"No."

"Kim Kardashian?"

"Close."

"Squeaky Fromme?"

"No! Get it right! It's fucking obvious!" Esmeralda bellowed.

I liked Esmeralda better in between psychotic episodes. "Paris Hilton?"

He was ecstatic. "Yes! Of course it's Paris Hilton."

I contemplated jumping off the tuk-tuk with Nok, and taking our chances with the monkeys and afflicted hordes.

"It's…beautiful," I said.

"You bet your ass it's beautiful. I saw her on the beach about two weeks ago. She had her little dog with her. So cute. Then I remembered there was a doctor here in Thailand that did facial transplants, so I asked if I could borrow hers."

My balls shrank up into a protective posture inside my stomach.

"And what'd she say?" I asked, realizing he was serious.

"She denied being Paris Hilton. She gave me some bullshit about being a celebrity lookalike that was doing a show. She said there were tons of celebrity impersonators here in town for some convention. I mean, can you believe I actually met Paris Hilton?"

I nodded again. "It seems you took a souvenir as well. Maybe it wasn't really her."

Esmeralda's eyes changed. I was starting to recognize the look that preceded one of his outbursts of psychosis.

"On second thought, you're probably right. Wow. You met *the* Paris Hilton. How 'bout that?"

"Goddamn fucking right I did. Now, I'm going to *be* Paris Hilton. Did you know she gets like a million dollars to go to a nightclub and have pictures taken of her?"

I nodded.

"She's the most beautiful and talented woman in the world. Now I'll get to go to movie premieres and fancy parties, and sleep with all kinds of sophisticated men, and I'll have all kinds of pretty dresses, and be famous, and..."

I thought this speech sounded familiar. It was from *Of Mice and Men*, when Lenny gets all excited about the rabbits.

I looked up to Vato as he maneuvered through the wrecked landscape of Kreungthep. He was taking this all in and looking over his shoulder. He called back to Esmeralda, "Hey, we gotta stop for gas, okay? Or we can just change to another tuk-tuk. I think I see one up ahead."

Esmeralda scanned the area through his rotting Paris Hilton mask. "Over there! That hotel has a nice one in front of it." He pointed to a four-star hotel, with a tuk-tuk parked out front. It looked brand new.

Vato pulled up to it and shut off the engine. He jumped out of ours, and ran up to the new one. "It doesn't have any keys."

"Go inside the hotel and look for them. We'll wait out here," Esmeralda told him.

"I ain't going in there. You go."

"Go inside you greasy wetback before I cut your fucking balls off!" Esmeralda snapped.

"Jai yen yen. Calm down, Miss Hilton," I said, patting his shoulder. "You wait here, and Nok and I will go inside to help him."

I nudged Nok to get out of the tuk-tuk.

"Monkey girl stays here with me," Esmeralda said. He had the look again, boiling up like a cauldron of insanity in his eyes.

"You're not keeping my wife as a hostage."

"You think I'm stupid? You don't think I know you are planning to run out the back exit of the hotel and go your own way?"

"No, Miss Hilton," I said and shook my head.

"Monkey girl stays here."

"You don't need to keep calling her that, you know? It's kinda rude."

Esmeralda grabbed one of Nok's arms and raised it up. "You see those bite marks? Do you know what happens to someone who gets bit by one of those monkeys?"

I gulped. I didn't have time to process the bite marks after being chased by a corpse-spewing vajayjay monster and watching a psychotic shemale with a bad toupee cutting off the heads of the undead while wearing the rotting face of a celebrity impersonator.

"Well, do you?"

"No. I don't"

"Neither do I, but the doctor I'm going to see can tend to her wounds and give her a shot or something," Esmeralda said. It made sense.

I looked at Nok. Her normally brown skin was turning a sickly shade of carnival-ride green. She hung her head low, as if she pulled inexorably into the long slow suck of sleep. The sun above hovered at an eternal noon, baking everything below into a tropic of death.

"Hurry boys," he said

Inside the hotel lobby, Vato and I came up with a plan. First, we had to snort a few lines of China and then we would see if the hotel bar had any booze. We lucked out. Vato came back with his arms full of Johnny Walker. We found the last remaining hotel staff member, frozen and catatonic behind the hotel bar. She was stunningly beautiful according to the Thai standards of white skin and high cheekbones.

"That's kind of high-end for Molotov's don't you think?" I said, pointing to the Johnny Walker.

"Nothing but the best for Miss Hilton. Wow, that hotel receptionist is hot. Did you see her?"

"Yeah , I saw her."

"You think maybe I can put her in the tuk-tuk with us? She'd be so grateful if we found a cure for her."

"She also may wake up and try to eat you," I said.

In a linen closet, we found a bunch of pillowcases and cut them into strips with our machetes. We stuffed them down into the neck of the bottles and wet them with the alcohol.

"Do you have a lighter?" Vato asked me.

I patted my pockets. There was one in my cigarette pack. "Yeah, I've got one. Who's gonna throw 'em?"

"You, man."

"No way. I had an epic fail with the grenade earlier. You throw."

"Fine. Gimme the lighter."

I handed Vato the lighter. "What's the plan again?"

"The plan is to get the psychotic fuck away from the tuk-tuk so we don't barbeque your girlfriend."

"Ah."

"You ready?" Vato asked.

"Hang on." I did one last line of China, and then for some reason, checked my nose in the mirror. "Let's do it."

Vato followed me to the hotel doors, but stayed inside the lobby. I took a deep breath and walked out into the oppressive sun. They were still there. Esmeralda held a pair of severed breasts up to his chest while checking himself out in the tuk-tuk's rearview mirror. He had taken off the Donald Trump toupee and traded it for a long, blonde wig. I didn't want to know what else he had in that cooler.

"Excuse me, Miss Hilton!" I called out.

Esmeralda put the breasts back in the cooler and turned towards me.

"There's a bunch of hot movie stars inside the hotel hiding out. I told them that I had Paris Hilton's body double outside, and they asked if you wanted to come join them. I think they want to get it on with you."

"Eww. That sounds gross. I'm a classy lady. Classy ladies like Paris Hilton don't go to parties like that. Did you get the keys?"

Esmeralda got out of the tuk-tuk and wiped off the brains and other bits of flesh hanging from his dress. "How do I look?"

"Beautiful."

Esmeralda left his axe by the tuk-tuk. In the life of a super-star, there was no need for violence. Esmeralda walked away from the tuk-tuk and adjusted the Paris-Hilton-impersonator mask. Vato must have gauged that Esmeralda was far enough away from Nok, because he burst out of the hotel's double doors and threw a lit bottle of Johnny Walker at him. His aim was better than mine. The bottle struck Esmeralda squarely in the forehead, breaking upon impact. The flames engulfed Esmeralda's hair and quickly spread to his flimsy dress. Esmeralda screamed in his raspy shemale voice until he inhaled the flame and the fire burned his alveoli. While the fire consumed him, he coughed and gurgled. His lungs sputtered, trying to find any trace of oxygen.

"Let's go!" I yelled to Vato.

Vato jumped into the driver's seat of the new tuk-tuk and pulled the keys from his pocket. Sneaky fucker. I went over and grabbed Nok. As I carried her back to the new tuk-tuk, her body was limp. I put her in the back seat, as Esmeralda did her death dance in the flames.

"We're in. Let's go!"

Vato had the hang of it now. He put the tuk-tuk in gear and revved away with ease from the hotel. I looked over my shoulder. Esmeralda was fully engulfed in flames. He staggered towards the hotel lobby, and then collapsed. I gave Nok a hug, and spotted Esmeralda's cooler on the seat. I reached over and flung it from the tuk-tuk. The Donald Trump toupee was still wedged into the seat. I pried the wig loose and examined it. The entire inside was made of wiring and computer chips. Around its circumference were small solenoids.

"What the fuck is this?" I asked Vato.

He was in another place. Vato's whole vibe was that of a homie on a stroll through a bucolic landscape of poppies and coca leaves. "Huh?" he said.

"This fucking Donald Trump hair-hat thing that the freak was wearing, it's full of wires and shit."

"Maybe it's from the loony bin. It's supposed to electro-shock his ass or something."

"I don't know. Should I toss it?"

"Up to you, bro. Unless you wanna wear it."

I chuckled. I think I was suffering from stress disorder. Or PTSD, only it wasn't the 'post' part yet. "Yeah man, how do I look?" I said, as I put the toupee on my head.

It started in the left side of my brain. A seizure of sorts. The electric numbness spread around my brain until my head no longer felt attached to my body. Then I saw them.

They darted from behind buildings in my peripheral vision. As we sped by, I saw them in the reflections of shop windows. They were coming through the glass of parked cars. Arms and heads crawling out. Black eyeballs and lolling tongues. There were too many different types to describe them as a collective species. One looked like a spider with the skin of a man, replete with veins and a human face. Another was a beautiful woman's head, connected to a body made entirely of entrails. Excrement dripped from the corners of her mouth as she smiled. As I passed her, she opened her mouth and vomited out a jet of half-masticated frogs. The tuk-tuk sped along, as day turned to night in a matter of seconds. There were shadows falling from the sky. They fell to the ground and took the form of another creature. I saw one fall into a bird's nest and emerge as a winged human – all of it swirling inside a nebulous cloud of filth and evil.

The only word that came to mind was demons.

I was screaming when Vato pulled the toupee from my head. He had stopped the tuk-tuk at the foot of the tollway to Pattaya. The first thing I saw was the abandoned tollbooth, the inside covered in blood. I shut my eyes against the sun. It was no longer nighttime. The images from the other world remained with me. Without an explanation, I understood it all. There was absolute knowledge, along with infinite horror. It was a place where I could view anything I wanted to see. Only I would have to be prepared to see *everything*.

"You okay, homie?" Vato asked. "Man, you were tripping balls."

"What-the-fuck-was-that?" I said. My brain felt as if it were hemorrhaging.

"You fell asleep and then woke up screaming. I think you need to do a line."

It sounded like a good idea. "Yeah, hit me with it."

Vato reached into his pocket and pulled out a small baggie of China with a cut straw sticking out as if from a juice box. "Here, bro," he said, handing it to me.

I took the baggie and jammed the straw up my nose, inhaling enough to kill Keith Richards. I sat back as the opiate spread its warmth through my body.

Nok moaned. I looked over at her. Her condition was getting worse by the hour. I was half expecting her to breathe one last breath and then awaken as one of the undead.

I expressed my concerns to Vato, and he told me I had seen too many movies. Until it actually happened, nothing was known. But this was Thailand, and the ghosts played by a whole set of different rules. The frog-vomit lady I'd seen was a Phii Krasue – widely known as the most feared ghost in Thailand. Phii Krasue fed on newborns, and when none were available, consumed shit and frogs. The Thais made incredibly dumb movies about her and featured her in commercials.

While wearing the toupee, I'd seen a mummified baby with gold leaf on his head. The images must have been coming from my subconscious mind because Nok and I had visited the temple of Mae Nak a few months before. In the temple's courtyard, the mummified baby was kept in a glass case. People came and offered toys to him and donated money through a slit in his coffin.

His face covered in gold leaf, he was revered because after death his body had barely decomposed.

"Throw that rat's nest away," Vato said.

I held the toupee in my hand and examined it again. A tag on one of the solenoids read: *Hencho en Mexico*.

I couldn't throw it away. Something about its power. I felt as if I should be skulking around Middle Earth with it.

"Hey, check it out," Vato said, as he picked up a nightclub flyer from the ground. "There's a punk band called Diarrhea Bukakke playing in Pattaya. They look Japanese."

I looked at the flyer. They did appear to be Japanese. "You like punk music?"

"Yeah, man, old school punk like The Germs and Minor Threat. How 'bout you?"

This reminded me of those moments in high school where your clique of friends was determined by your mutual taste in music. The guy could be a total shitheel, but at least he listened to The Clash. "Yeah, man. I grew up in Hermosa Beach. There was a big punk scene back in the day."

"For reals? I'm from East Los, bro. You're a Cali boy, too?"

"Yep. Born and raised."

"So why didn't you say so in the first place?"

"Didn't think it mattered. Besides, I come here to get away from other Americans."

"I feel you. I first came to Bangkok and saw all these fine-ass ladies who weren't all stuck-up and I was like damn, I gotta move here. Youknowwhatimsayin?"

Vato and I reminisced about the finer points of California life. Besides riding unicorns and watching yoga instructors mediate on Venice Beach, we recalled California's more resplendent features such as its borderline psychotic drivers – who were often armed – and its beautiful, self involved women, who wouldn't talk to you unless you were a millionaire. Then there was the endless parade of delusional and talentless fuckwads that came from all corners of the globe to be movie stars. Most ended up as waiters. Some ended up as crack whores. The very few got a gig in a porno or rap video, barely making enough for a bus ticket back home.

"How you feeling now? You done freaking out?" Vato asked.

I was feeling better and said so. Nok was looking pretty bad. I thought of dumping her on the side of the road. If it weren't for her looks, I would have left her a long time ago. Then again, she was capable of tolerating me for more than five consecutive minutes – something no other woman could do. Until we got to a doctor, I would keep her with me. If the prognosis was bad, then I wouldn't feel guilty about leaving her to the monkeys.

"We gotta try and get my girl to a doctor. There's gotta be something like a hospital that's not crawling with the afflicted."

"I know of a place near Pattaya called Banglamung Hospital. I was there a few years ago after I got into a fight on the beach," Vato said, rolling up his sleeve to show a scar from stitches.

"Doctors have probably run off, though. Maybe nobody raided the pharmacy yet. We can just give her a cocktail of different shit and see what works. That's all doctors do anyhow. They're a bunch of quacks."

I agreed. As we got ready to leave, a sleeper reanimated in the back of a minivan. It started flipping out as it tried to figure out how to exit the vehicle and eat us. Vato grabbed an old newspaper lying on the ground and walked up to the minivan. He opened its gas tank while the sleeper clawed at the glass and made its retarded death faces.

"Man this bitch looks hungry, yo. Check it out, she's like only seven years old."

Vato took the newspaper and stuffed it into the gas tank. He pulled out the lighter I'd given him and lit the paper. Before sprinting back over to me, Vato stood in front of the window and waved goodbye to the sleeper.

"We should really go check out that band in Pattaya, huh?" he said.

I glanced over Vato's shoulder at the sleeper in the minivan. She was indeed only seven or so years old. She wore a shirt that was among my favorites in Thailand. It was one of the many knockoffs of superhero shirts. This one showed a man in tights swinging down from a building – but his outfit was green and his name was Spaderman. I wanted to ask the now-convulsing and rabid little girl if she had ever seen the movie in the theater or only as a bootleg DVD camcorder job.

My questions would go unanswered, as the gas tank caught fire and the whole minivan exploded in a whoosh. The girl's head flew into the air, spinning end over end, with its jaw moving and eyes rolling around. The head landed on the street a few yards away. Its eyes fixed on us as if there were still the possibility of taking a bite.

We got back in the tuk-tuk and entered the elevated toll road to Pattaya. It was the same as the streets in the city – mile after mile of abandoned cars with no passengers inside or sleepers yet to awaken. In the panic that had swept the city, people had tried to escape. The hoods and insides of the cars were covered with blood, documenting their owners' last moments of a violent death. Blood spatter painted the road at regular intervals, transforming the land into an abstract hellscape.

We drove for about thirty minutes, while I studied the toupee. Every moment I held it filled me with the temptation to put it back on. Right in front of us, there was a world that we could not see. With the toupee on my head, I could know everything about the universe. All of life's mysteries and riddles would be answered. All I had to do was put it back on and see the show.

The desire to see what lies beyond overwhelmed me, and I began to raise the toupee to my head. Vato spotted me in the rearview mirror, reached around, and snatched the toupee from my hands. He flung it out of the tuk-tuk and revved the engine as we raced between cars.

"What the fuck, man?" I said.

"Homie, you're acting like fucking Golem with that thing. Give it up. We got more important shit to worry about. You wanna end up like Esmeralda back there?'

He was right. I shook my head.

"So get your head on straight and watch out for the afflicted. There's bound to be some on this road at some point."

"I'm cool, man. No worries. Can you hand me the baggie again?"

Vato handed me the baggie with the straw and told me to keep it. We drove on with the tuk-tuk's engine buzzing like a cloud of mosquitoes. Pattaya was two hours away from Bangkok. I had only been there twice, and had had a great time and a miserable one. Pattaya was an adult Disneyland where many men went to die – or at least go out with a bang. It had an image as a Sodom by the sea – a place where old white guys shagged young Thai girls. In recent years, the crowd had changed. Now it was just as common to see young hipsters. The bullshit in the city grew exponentially with its wealth. Jet Ski scam artists fleeced tourists for pre-existing damage. Clip joints overcharged, and women bled punters for their life savings. Left with nothing, many of the men jumped from the city's high-rises, turning "balcony diving" into a national sport. I couldn't think of a better place to live at the end of the world.

"Rigor mortis Death Queef," Vato said to me over his shoulder as he drove. It took me a few moments to process it.

"Say what?"

Vato held up the flyer from the bar he had showed me earlier.

"They're opening up for Diarrhea Bukakke."

"Yeah? They Japanese too?'

Vato's eyes darted to the flyer in between zigzagging around road debris.

"I dunno. I think they might be a ladyboy punk band. Fucking Japanese are freaks man. You ever watch Japanese porn?"

I had, of course. "Yeah, who hasn't?"

"They're into all that rape and scat porn man. Fucking deviants. The Japanese girls all cry like wounded puppies in those movies too. I have to watch them on mute."

Vato had determined that he should at least make an effort to locate the Ka Yai mobsters and try to return the bag full of China – albeit, a few ounces lighter now. It would be an act of good faith. If they were dead or missing, he would be free to bury his face in it daily, or sell it, barter it, even throw it on the floor and make snow angels in it.

"You ever see the series *Groped by Gorbechev*?" he said

"Is that on the BBC?"

"It's a Russian porn series. I don't really know the premise of it, but the cats that shoot it live down in Pattaya now. They've got this huge-ass mansion in town with ten-foot walls, gates, security and shit. I'll bet you anything that they are riding this thing out in style."

Over the years, the Russian expat community had grown huge. They tended to treat Thailand the way Americans treated Mexico. It didn't endear them to the locals.

"They've got a whole smut series with a Soviet theme. Some shit like *Licked by Lenin, Bolshevik Butt Buddies, KGBJ',s* and whatnot. It's pretty cheesy stuff, but I'll bet their pad is stock-piled with dope and fine-ass ladies."

"You thinking about joining them?"

Vato shrugged, "I'm just sayin."

Pattaya was an entire city of go-go bars, massage parlors, and brothels. To cater to the punters, it had malls, movie theaters, and Western restaurants. Over the years, people had attempted to make it into a "family place." I could never wrap my head around that one or understand why families would want to drag their brood down Walking Street. *Look son, next to that Roman-style orgy venue is a statue of Buddha, and another one of Ganesh. You see, son, Thai bargirls are very devout. They often pray to not only the Buddha, but also to the spirits of dead children called Phii Dek, which is the ghost of a dead child whose mother probably killed him. If the gods or ghosts bring a customer to the bargirl, then she has to make an offering. That's what those toys and fruits in front of the statue are for. One out of four girls here has HIV, and they continue to work even though they might infect a customer. Well, son, that completes today's multicultural learning experience. When you are old enough, you can go to the bars and catch herpes, too.*

The tuk-tuk sped down the tollway while Vato and I tried to fill the moments of silence by getting to know each other better. We spoke of the world back home as if it were an idealized snowy Swiss village. The truth was we hated it, and that is how we ended up here. We were both convinced that America would become a Third World country some day, and that places such as Thailand, Brazil, and even parts of genocide-ridden Africa would eventually rise up to claim their places in the sun. Our talk went from politics to porno movies, and where to get the best hummers in Pattaya.

Vato confided in me that he was on the run. There was an Interpol warrant out for one Ramón Rodriguez. He didn't look like a Ramón. He didn't seem much concerned about the warrant either. He had surrendered to apathy about the situation and planned to make money as long as he could to stay ahead of the authorities. Life on the lam had never been glamorous. There was no beach with margarita in hand – only a life of disposable cell phones and prepaid credit cards. A life spent avoiding pen registers and nervous waits in customs lines. It was the life of a blank. It was the wet dream of so many hustlers, robbers, and grifters. How many had planned the perfect score, only to be handcuffed on a Phuket beach while screaming to the high heavens that they had the wrong man?

Vato was a walking database on foreign intelligence agencies and their exploits. He loved talking about the cyanide in the toothpaste method, or the ricin pellet injected under the skin trick. Vato insisted that the true artists in the genre were the Mossad. To them, assassinations were a form of creative expression. He claimed to have worked with, supplied dope to, and been trained by some of the world's finest alphabet agencies. He would often point to people passing on the street and label them: DST, MI6, CIA, and whatever the KGB was calling itself these days. He changed hotels weekly, sometimes nightly. He went low-tech, and practiced the old-school tradecraft on which the various groups had become lazy with the advances in electronic spying.

Vato had a marketable skill. He was incredibly good at tolerating bullshit. It was equal parts talent and art – a needed skill in his line of work. The gods have their pincushions. They needed them. Through endless ordeals, they sifted them out of the rest of the population. They looked for a sap living a joyless fucking existence, and take it from there – heaping it on. Seeing how far they can push in the blade until you cry. They throw you down a well just to see if you dive in or cling to the walls as you fall. Either way, you go down to the bottom.

Vato had, like so many other men in Thailand, found redemption in the arms of a woman. He waxed on about her for the better part of twenty minutes, until he pulled out a picture from his wallet. The woman in the photo looked as if someone had hit her in the face with a shovel, and then tried to cover the wreckage with blue eye shadow and garish lipstick. Vato and Shovel Face, I thought. There should be a constellation named after them. The beast and the harlot were as old a match as time itself.

"Pretty girl," I told him.

We passed car after car full of sleepers and afflicted. Several had managed to escape their vehicles and were staggering down the road. Before they knew we were there, we were already gone. We were in survival mode, not on a military search-and-destroy mission. Avoiding them was good enough.

I saw one afflicted lady that reminded me of Nok. She wore a Hello Kitty shirt and walked along, dragging her intestines on the ground behind her. We were effectively in a war zone, and an overwhelming sense of freedom overtook me. There would be no more bills to pay. No more job to show up to. A man's worth would be measured by how well he could swing a machete and by whatever he could manage to loot.

Now, Nok's carnival ride green skin was turning blue. I wondered if I could love her as a corpse. If she turned into one of the afflicted that roamed the city, I would like to follow her around at a distance just to study her daily life. I might even find a survivor or two and feed them to her. My role as a good provider would extend even beyond death. Part of me longed to see her chasing someone down the street in a blood frenzy, tackling the hapless retard who crossed her path. I would cheer her on saying shit like, "You go girl!" or "Oh no she didn't!"

"We've got trouble," Vato said. Ahead on the toll road was a minivan with a fat woman on the roof. Surrounding it was what seemed to be a group of children or possibly little people. Vato pulled over the tuk-tuk and turned off the engine. "We're almost out of gas anyway, man. This could be bad."

The minivan was about a hundred yards down the road. I looked at the endless line of cars around us. Some of the bodies were gone. Others had sleepers in them. A few of the cars had occupants that had already awakened and become afflicted. Apparently they were too stupid to figure out how the door handles worked on their cars, so they simply licked the windows and stared at us.

"What do you think, man?" I asked Vato.

He lit a cigarette and took a snort from another baggie in his pocket. "Only one way there. This road eventually ends up on ground level. It's elevated like this for just a little bit more. I don't see any tuk-tuks ahead, do you?"

I looked down the length of the highway. It was all bumper-to-bumper traffic with cars and minivans. "No, man. Do you wanna see what's going on up ahead? That fat lady might need some help."

"Not really. I didn't get this far by helping people."

"You helped me, and you're helping me now," I said.

We stared at each other for a minute, then grabbed our machetes and walked towards the minivan. We crouched low behind the abandoned cars, as we got closer to the scene. A woman on the wrong side of fifty was standing on top of a mauve-colored minivan. Surrounding her were around a dozen kids who had already become afflicted. Judging by their height, I guessed them to be no more than seven years old. Since this was Thailand, that probably meant ten. The kids seemed to be sobbing. It was the mournful cry that children let out when they went to bed without supper. The woman seemed exhausted. She held a book in one hand and clutched onto a necklace with the other. She mumbled to herself in what was obviously a prayer.

"They're just kids. You think we can take 'em without getting bit?" Vato asked me.

"Fuck if I know. I'm not exactly keen on chopping up children."

"They're not children. They're afflicted."

"Same same but different?"

Vato nodded, "Exactly."

I paused and felt my heart racing. I felt constipated. I needed stool softeners to offset the bowel paralyzing effects of doing so many opiates. My face must have shown it.

"What's the matter?" Vato asked me

"My heart's racing," I told him. "I should go back to the tuk-tuk and get my Xanax."

"Nah, try this…Bear down like you're taking a shit. Grunt really hard for ten seconds. It lowers your heart rate. Trust me. I do it when I pass through customs if I'm nervous."

"Seriously?"

"Yeah man, I'll do it with you okay? Ready? Let's go."

Vato started grunting as if he was pinching out a huge loaf. His face turned red and veins began popping out of his temples. He motioned with his hand for me to hurry up and join him, if there was such a hand sign. I grunted a little and felt lightheaded. I tried again and held it. I could feel my face becoming flush and pressure building up in my eyeballs. Vato nodded and gave me the thumbs up. Before I could stop it from coming, a huge, rock-hard turd shot out of my ass.

"Fuck!" I shouted.

"What's up bro? Did it work?'

"Yeah it fucking worked. I shit my pants."

"Dumbass, you're supposed to bear down, not actually shit yourself."

"You didn't say that."

"It's a vagal maneuver. I thought it was obvious."

I was wearing boxers. I could feel the turd starting to move. It was now directly under my balls. "Fuck!" I shouted again, as I put down my machete and reached into the front of my pants. I fished around until I had my hand on it, when Vato backhanded me lightly on the shoulder.

"Um, hey dude," Vato whispered.

"Fuck! What?"

"Look up."

When I looked up, I still had my hand down the front of my pants holding onto the turd. The group of afflicted children stood on the opposite side of the cars – glaring at us. They wore name-tags in the shape of hearts cut from construction paper. One named Fon was staring at me. Half of her face was missing from bite wounds. Her lips were gone, exposing her blood-covered teeth – which I assumed meant she had already claimed a victim.

I made a decision to continue with my turd extraction. It was part of some deeply embedded desire not to be found dead with crap in my pants. Back home, the same desire had led me into an agreement with a buddy that if one of us died, the other would go to the deceased's apartment and throw away all of the dead guy's porn collection before his mom could find it.

Vato jumped up and looked around. We were along the guardrail. On one side were cars and afflicted children, and on the other side a thirty-foot fall. He took off sprinting in the direction of Pattaya. He got about twenty feet and then stopped and turned around. He began to job back at a leisurely pace. The afflicted children followed him with their eyes.

"Forgot your bag?" I asked.

"Yep."

"So what do we do?"

The bumper-to-bumper traffic created a continual barrier as far as the eye could see. So far, none of the afflicted had attempted to climb over the vehicles that separated us. I didn't want to be around when they figured out how.

"Hey lady!" Vato yelled to the woman on top of the minivan.

She was still mumbling with her eyes closed.

"What a retard," I said.

Vato chuckled and looked at me. I was holding the turd in my right hand.

"Throw that at her. Get her attention," he said.

I looked past the faces of the afflicted children to the woman. I held out my left arm as a sighting mechanism and let it fly. The afflicted children followed the flight of the turd with their heads. Their demeanor was that of a lazy cat that had just seen a ball roll by. My turd hit her in the face, and she let out a yelp. It bounced off of her cheek and tumbled down her chest, where it picked up height from her boobs like a ski lift, and then settled on top of the book in her hand. My aim was improving.

"Nice shot," Vato said. He held his hand up for a high five.

I left him hanging on the high five as my attention was fixed on the afflicted children. Several of them were no longer visible.

"Where's the chick with her lips bit off?" I asked Vato.

"Who?"

"Fon, the chick, I mean the little girl with half her fucking face missing."

"Beats me," Vato said.

We both looked down. A tiny arm was poking out from under the car and reaching for Vato's foot. I raised my machete and brought it down on the arm – severing it at the elbow. I'd expected arterial spray, but a viscous substance oozed out of her arm. The child didn't seem to mind, as it continued to crawl out from under the car. To our right and left, more afflicted children were emerging from below the other vehicles.

I jumped up on top of the car, and one of the afflicted children reached out to snatch one of my ankles. I needed to get to higher ground, so I ran down the length of the parked cars and hopped from one vehicle to the next. I could hear Vato behind me jumping on the car hoods. I didn't see any minivans on our side of the road. When I looked around, I saw the horde of afflicted children staggering towards us. I jumped down into the road and hopped over the other row of cars. Vato was a beat behind me and when he jumped almost went over the side of the elevated road.

"What now, fuckhead?" Vato said.

"I don't wanna leave Nok. I'm gonna run back to the fat lady."

"Bro, we should–"

I was already sprinting.

"Wait up, homie," I heard Vato say.

I made it back to the mauve minivan. The woman hadn't moved. She was still mumbling to herself with her eyes closed. I hopped up on top of the hood and clambered up to the top of the van. This was one of the jumbo-style passenger vans seen throughout Thailand – the kind that sat eight people, but were often crammed with double that number. I stood next to the fat woman and looked down at her book. It was, in fact, a Bible. It still had my turd on top of it.

Vato jumped up onto the hood and then climbed up with us. The horde of afflicted children was coming back. Their movements were slow and labored. Those who had crawled beneath the cars were now returning to join the others. I saw Fon again. I had cut off her arm and for some reason felt sorry for her. That pity was gone the moment I saw the blood around her mouth.

"Good job, ace," Vato said.

I looked back at the fat woman and shook her shoulder. She whined a little but continued in her prayers. She had gigantic tits, which were held up by an industrial strength 1950s-style bra.

"Hey!" I shouted at her.

No response. She wore a floral-patterned shirt that flared at the bottom, in an apparent attempt to hide her sizable gut, which was almost as big as her boobs. A subtle, yet ostentatious crucifix hung between them. Her flabby grandma arms jiggled in syncopation with her fear tremors.

I looked at her Bible and t a thought entered my head. It was, quite possibly, the worst idea I'd had all day.

"Dude, help me take her shirt off," I told Vato.

"Say what?"

"I want to take her bra and use it as a slingshot."

Vato chuckled. When he laughed, he sounded like a stoner.

"Seriously, homes?"

"Yeah man, rapido."

I stepped around the fat woman and lifted up the back of her shirt. She had on granny panties that were pulled up over her midsection – cleverly disguising the rolls of fat, which smelled like bad cheese.

"Goddamn this mama is thick," Vato said.

"Don't molest her; just help me lift her shirt up."

"I gotta get rid of her Bible first."

Vato pulled at the woman's Bible, and the turd plunked to the ground. Her grip was tight on her holy book and she wouldn't let go. As Vato tried to pry her fingers away, the woman raised her right hand and punched him in the jaw. She had a lot of center mass. If she would have put her hips into it, I'm sure she would have knocked him out.

"Rape!" she screamed.

I backed away and she turned to me, Bible raised. She began beating me with the good book. I blocked most of her shots with my arms, but one got through and smacked me in the nose. Right away, my eyes began tearing up.

"Grab her, man!" I yelled to Vato.

He paused, then snaked his arms through hers and wrapped her in a full nelson. The woman sidestepped with ease and got her legs behind Vato's. I could see the *what the fuck?* expression on his face as she bent down, snatched up his leg, and reverse body slammed him into the roof of the van.

"Fat bitch is a pro wrestler. Get her off of me!" Vato cried.

"Miss. Calm down okay? Nobody's trying to rape you."

Her face changed from fear to rage. "What the fuck are you cocksuckers trying to do to me? Perverts! I'll kill you like I did my ex-husband!"

"We just need your bra ma'am. I saw your Bible, and I thought of David and Goliath. I wanted to use it as a sling to kill the afflicted."

"Fucking punks! I'll tear your balls off and shove 'em up your ass!"

The woman had taken Vato's back, and was applying a rear naked choke. His face began turning red. "Do something," he coughed.

I raised my machete over her head. "Ma'am, please! Let him go, or you'll force me to kill you. I just need your bra."

"Cocksucker motherfuckers!" she screamed. As she yelled, white spittle shot out of her mouth. She had her forearm around Vato's trachea. It was a more painful choke than having your carotid artery squeezed. Vato made gurgling sounds as his eyes rolled back into his head.

I closed my eyes and brought the machete down RUF guerilla style. I felt the metal hit her skull and then slide down the side of her head. The woman shrieked. When I opened my eyes, I saw I had sliced off her left ear. The woman let go of Vato and stood up. She held her left hand to her ear, and raised the other one in a fist.

"Stay back. I'm warning you," I told her.

The woman lunged at me in an apparent attempt at a double

leg take down. *She is a wrestler*, I thought. To fend her off, I accidentally brought the machete upwards to her face. The machete bit into her chin and then continued on – cutting off her lips. She screamed again. Blood ran down her flowery shirt and soaked her undulating belly.

"Don't kill her!" Vato shouted.

I was terrified. The damage had been done. I was about to become a murderer. I had sliced off her ear and her lips. She wouldn't be able to continue on like this. There was no medical care nearby, and I couldn't imagine her riding to Pattaya with us to find a doctor. It was best to put her out of her misery. The woman fell to her knees and covered her mouth with her hands. The human body triaged pain, and I gathered from this that the wound to her mouth hurt more than her ear. I stood over her and raised my machete. The woman coughed on the blood running down her throat and looked up at me. I saw something in the whites of her eyes. *Something swimming.*

The old woman began to laugh, "All you faggots are going to die!" she said. Blood gargled in the back of her throat as she continued to spit out a string of obscenities. The things swimming in her eyes looked like worms, and they darted back and forth as though searching for a way out. The woman continued to laugh like a maniac, as the things in her eyes moved faster. I could see them crawling under the skin of her face towards her severed ear. A moment later, they emerged from the ear cavity and turned what I believed to be their heads in different direction.

Vato got back to his feet and retrieved his machete. He maneuvered around the woman and stood next to me. I glanced down at the road. All of the afflicted children were motionless, their eyes transfixed on the old lady. I could see the same worms in the eyes of the child nearest to me.

"What is it?" Vato asked.

"How in the fuck should I know?"

"Is it a worm?"

"Looks like one."

The woman's head began to convulse and her eyes rolled back. I saw more movement under the skin on her face. This time, they were moving in all directions. Boils began forming on her head as the worms tried to push their way out. Her hair moved as the ones under her scalp also searched for an exit. I looked down at the afflicted children and they too were convulsing, their bodies writhing in full body spasms. Like a thousand infected hemorrhoids exploding at once, the worms shot out from the boils on the woman's head. They stood up in the air about two feet, and thrashed around and around. To an extent, she resembled a fat Gorgon.

I looked back at the afflicted children. As they convulsed, the worms inside of them began boiling up. Then, as if in sync, the worms exploded from their heads in the same manner as they had the woman's. The afflicted children fell to the ground. Vato and I stared slack-jawed and watched as the worms detached from their hosts and scurried off underneath the cars. My gaze returned to the woman. Her face was contorted in pain. The worms that emerged from her scalp had spiked barbs along their bodies, and they were covered with bits of the woman's brain. I looked into her eyes and could see that she was dead. Her body fell back onto the roof of the van, and the worms detached themselves from her head. They slithered over the side of the van and disappeared from sight.

There was no sound except for our adrenaline-fueled breathing. Not even a call from a bird, nor the rustling of the wind. It seemed as though the whole world had died and left nothing in its will.

"Wow. That was fucking metal," I said

Vato looked at me, "You still want her bra?"

We looked around at the scene: Dead children and a fat woman with holes in their heads from parasites. I'm not very smart, but this one was obvious.

"She was some kind of a trap," I said. "They were waiting for someone to come along and help the fat lady, and either the kids would get us or the fat lady would."

"Yeah, man. They're probably all interconnected and shit. She's like the controller, and those worms took off when the main host died."

We knew it was parasites. The only thing keeping them from taking over our minds was the drugs.

"I'm such a dumbass," I said.

"Sup man?"

"We've been getting fucked up this whole time, and Nok hasn't. If we've all got the parasites inside of us already, then we just need to give more drugs to Nok."

"Maybe, but she got bit by a monkey. They might have something else in them like monkey AIDS," Vato said.

"If she lives long enough to die from monkey AIDS, I'd be happy. I may as well just give her an overdose and send her off with a smile on her face."

I jogged back to where we'd left Nok. She was asleep in the back of the tuk-tuk. I tried to wake her by yelling, shaking, and some light slapping. Nothing worked. I asked Vato for his baggie and went to work tying to rub some on her gums.

"There's other ways to get that inside of her, you know?"

"You got a syringe?"

Vato looked through his bag. "I've got a box of them. I busted into a medical center and took some necessities before I ran into you. Need any steroids?"

"No thanks. Why would you take steroids when there's so much other shit to take?" I asked.

Vato looked at me as if I were a total newb. "I was told to meet the Ka Yai in Pattaya. Its gonna be full of Jarheads, Navy squids, and about a thousand horny old men. I took what I thought I could barter. Mainly Viagra and steroids. Those Jarheads especially will want some roids."

"Whatever. Can you show me how to do this? I've never shot someone up before."

Vato used an old aluminum can instead of a spoon, and the stuffing out of a kid's toy in lieu of cotton. After tying her arm with my belt, I slapped it to get a vein. Vato handed me the syringe. I took it from him and did my best not to fuck it up. When I released the belt, the effect was almost immediate.

Nok's face came back to life little by little.

"Give her some more, man," Vato said.

"She's gonna overdose."

"Have you overdosed yet? You've done more than enough to kill an elephant. This shit is just leveling us out."

"You're right. Fix me up another," I told him.

We gave Nok three more shots, until she finally opened her eyes and yawned. She seemed quite refreshed.

"Oi. Where we go?" she asked.

I stroked her hair and kissed her nose. My world was far more interesting with her alive in it.

"We go to Pattaya. Pattaya not very far more," I said.

"Bro, you talk to her like she's a fob," Vato said.

"It helps her understand."

"What fob mean?" Nok asked.

"It mean you fresh off the boat," I told her.

"What boat?" she asked. "I don't take boat."

"See what you started?" I told Vato.

"Where the crazy guy who dress like pooying?" Nok asked.

"He's dead. We burned him with fire."

Nok stood up and stretched her legs. She looked down the road full of parked and abandoned cars. "Oi, have big big rot tit," she said.

"Huh?" said Vato.

"She just said there's a lot of traffic. She mixes her Thai and English."

"We go walking, na?" Nok said.

"Let's go, man," I said to Vato.

"Let me grab my shit. I guess we can find another ride up ahead."

We walked past the scene with the fat woman and decided to take a look in the van. We found some bottled water and bags of chips. Many cars were stocked with supplies. In the gridlock, there was simply no place to go. We'd had a nice, new tuk-tuk, but when it ran out of gas we opted to treat it like a disposable lighter. In hindsight, it was plain dumb. Siphoning off gas would have been a much better idea, but we didn't have a hose or a gas can and we were too lazy to look. Now we had walked a mile and still no more tuk-tuks.

"Let's turn back and get the tuk-tuk. I don't see any more up ahead. We just need to get some gas," I said.

"Yes. It very hot. You go get. I wait here," Nok said.

"There's probably one down the road a little ways. Just gotta keep walking," Vato added.

I jumped up on one of the parked cars and scanned the line of vehicles. There weren't any tuk-tuks. I turned around and looked in the area we'd just passed through – and thought I saw something moving just out of the corner of my eye. But whenever I turned, it was gone.

"You're right. I'm getting a bad vibe. Like there's something following us. Let's keep going," I said.

Nok bitched and moaned, moaned and bitched, but that was common for her, especially when it was hot. Even though she'd grown up here, she'd never adjusted to the heat.

We slouched along under the oppressive sun, passing cars with sleepers and afflicted inside. Vato amused himself by stuffing newspaper inside the gas tanks and setting them on fire. But he stopped when we passed a car with an afflicted infant inside. There were two car seats, which meant the family wasn't Thai – a the Thai had no problem strapping a newborn onto the gas tank of a motorcycle and racing through traffic. Car seats were a safety precaution only a farang would care about. One of the car seats was empty and covered in blood. The afflicted infant that survived had apparently eaten his sibling. As he looked through the car window at the baby, Vato was enthralled.

"How's that even possible? The kid's like ten months old. He probably hardly has any teeth," Vato said.

"I don't know, man. Why don't you stick your hand through the window and find out?" I told him.

On the other side of the car, Vato had his face up to the glass and the baby did, too. "Cute little guy," he said, opening the gas tank and stuffing newspaper inside.

I cackled – something about the gallows humor of it all. Surrounded by death and horror, it was common for people to make fun of corpses – the way soldiers did in war. Every time there something awful to contemplate, I reacted by cracking up.

"You're gonna tell the baby he's cute and then set him on fire? That's so monumentally fucked up. Why don't you at least club him in the head and give him a less painful death?" I said.

"Listen, douche. In case you didn't notice, hitting them in the head doesn't totally work. Remember those worms that popped out of the fat lady when you hit her? You gotta burn them and destroy the whole creature. This isn't a fucking zombie movie."

I turned away. Nok was a devout Buddhist and prayed for the soul of every dead body we saw. Vato burning the baby disturbed her more than anything that had happened so far.

"Baby going to become Phii Dek," she said.

"I know. Just pray to Buddha for him and maybe he be okay," I told her.

"What the fuck's a Phii Dek?" Vato asked.

"Nothing to worry about. Just a ghost baby that will probably haunt you the rest of your life," I said.

Ignoring us, Vato lit the newspaper, and we walked down the road. About thirty seconds later, the gas tank caught fire and exploded. Cars around it caught fire – and when I turned I saw smoke rising from the twenty or so cars Vato had already burned. Long black columns of smoke wafted into the air. We may have just as well taken out an ad telling people where we are.

"We should probably cool it with the car burning, man. You're letting the afflicted know our location," I said to Vato.

"You might have told me twenty cars ago."

"It just occurred to me."

We walked another thirty minutes, and the road started to slope down where it met ground level again. The traffic was still gridlocked. Everybody, it seemed, had the same idea to leave town. Bangkok's normal traffic was epic, putting to shame anything I had ever bitched about in Los Angeles. During a crisis, the roads in Thailand turned into a parking lot.

"Get ready to be happy, gang. I think I see something up ahead with three wheels," I said.

"Where all the tuk-tuk go?" Nok asked.

"The tuk-tuks and the scooters are the only things that could navigate this gridlock. They're probably gone," I told her.

"Arai na?"

I was forgetting to put it in her language. "Too many car. Car too big to go. Tuk-tuk and motorcycle very small. They can go more. Kao jai mai?" I said

She nodded. "Yes I understand."

We walked down the highway ramp to the very bottom. Vato spotted the three-wheeled rickshaw and ran up to it. I could see him jumping up and down. As I got closer, I realized it wasn't happiness but rage.

"Its pedal-powered man. Goddamnit," he said.

"Wow. Really? That blows," was all I could say.

"Fuck it. Let's just take it until we find something else."

Vato seemed to be losing it. I didn't want to break his heart, but something needed to be said.

"It has flat tires, man," I told him.

Vato looked down and began to sob. He started crying for his mother in Spanish.

"Jai yen yen. It okay. We find another one, na?" Nok said to him.

Vato pulled out the baggie from his pocket and started doing monster lines of H.

"Why there nobody here?" Nok asked

I looked around. It was, indeed, a wasteland.

"Probably because all of the afflicted have gone to Pattaya. They're probably drawn to more urban areas," I said.

"Arai na?"

I slapped my forehead. This got old after a while. "Many people go to city. No people here because nothing for them to eat. The dead people want to eat more people so they walk that way," I added, pointing towards Pattaya. Nok seemed satisfied with my explanation.

"Listen, man, I'm sorry this turned into such a cluster fuck. Just think of all that sweet Thai booty you'll get once we're in Pattaya," I said.

Nok punched my shoulder. She understood that, at least.

"Honey, we can take rice plow. One over there," Nok said.

I looked to my right. I had seen it before, but had ruled it out because I had no idea how it worked.

"Can you drive it?" I asked her.

"Yes, can."

"Sweet. You see, man, it's all good now," I told Vato.

Nok handled the plow with ease. Growing up on a farm near Cambodia had resulted in a skill set most survivalists would envy. She could start a fire with sticks, spot fruit in the trees from far away, and if I wanted a coconut, she would just kick off her flip-flops and climb a tree like a monkey. She was the girl you would want to be stranded on an island with.

This plow was basically an engine on top of extremely raked out front forks. The only thing I could compare it to was a Mad-Max custom chopper, mated with a Third-World tractor. We sat in the back while Nok rode on its horse-and-carriage-style bench seat. She steered the motorcycle-type handlebars and got the thing off road. This beast was designed to pull through rice fields. It had no problem handling the ground off the highway.

"Where I go?" Nok yelled over the noise of the engine.

"Just keep going straight. Dtrong bpai."

For the better part of an hour, we drove until the outskirts of the Pattaya conurbation came into view. Death had settled over the landscape like a shroud. The random afflicted wandered the streets. As Nok drove up next to one, Vato and I hacked it with our machetes. Until I got the kinks in my killing technique ironed out, I practiced different strokes. I swung the heavy Thai machete, catching the afflicted at the base of the skull, slicing the head off clean. By the tenth kill, my hands started to blister. This was how I imagined ancient chariot warfare – which gave me a totally bitchin' idea.

"Yo. Do you know what a scythed chariot was?" I asked Vato.

"Maybe. Refresh my memory," he said.

"The ancient Persians used them. It's just a chariot with blades attached to the wheels. You drive through a crowd and it cuts people's legs off."

"So?"

"So…That would be fucking metal right? We could turn this rice plow into an apocalypse death machine. You know, deck it out with chainsaws and spikes all over it. Some killer fuckin blades on the wheels and then we could just roll through the city. It would be badass," I said.

Vato looked at me the way a psychiatrist does to a patient who has just said he can talk to Kenny Rogers on his microwave.

"Yeah, that's great and everything. Sounds like quite a project," Vato said.

"Lets do it, man!" I said. I guess I came across as way too excited.

Vato spoke to me in a slow, steady voice. "You know that guy at the party who does way too much coke and starts coming up with all kinds of great ideas of shit to do but just sits there and does more coke?"

"Yeah."

"You're becoming that guy."

The afflicted's numbers were growing. After hitting them, the worms inside their heads would explode through giant boils. We saw sleepers, as well. The afflicted left the sleepers alone. They only attacked people who…

"I'm confused," I told Vato. "Check it out, we've all got these parasites in us, right?'

"Uh huh."

"And the rage that takes over when you're not on drugs makes you attack someone else?"

"Right. I guess."

"Then that person becomes a sleeper and awakens as one of the afflicted, right?"

"You're very observant, yes," Vato said.

"Then the afflicted attack someone else and that one becomes a sleeper and so on."

"Who cares, man? What's your point?"

"My point is…hang on…shit, I forgot what I was going to say."

Nok drove the rice plow, and we hacked at a few more afflicted. Up ahead, I saw the hotels that lined Beach Road. To the right was the ocean. More and more afflicted were walking around. In the distance, I heard gunshots.

"Fuck yeah, man! High five," Vato said.

I high-fived him.

"That was lame. Once more with feeling, bro."

I smacked the shit out of his hand. The hand slapping was hard enough to make us both wince.

"Check it out. I remember now," I said.

"Who cares, man? We are fucking *here,* bro," Vato patted Nok on the shoulder. "Good driving, babe," he said.

"These parasites are evolving. I think they may even be mating when they make contact with another person." I said. I was talking fast, trying to get my point across.

"Whatever, man," Vato said. "I'm gonna lock myself in a

room for a month with an eight-ball of cocaine, a case of whiskey, and about nine or ten Thai girls."

"Look, man, this is important. I had tapeworm last year. It freaked me the fuck out to know I had a parasite living in me. All this Thai street food I eat, not to mention the shit I eat out in the countryside, it's literally laden with parasites. I went to the pharmacy and they gave me Albendazole. It killed the worm, but it made me want to read a bunch of stuff about it–"

"You're really a killjoy aren't you, man? I don't want to hear about your butt worms."

"Dickhole, listen to me for a second. I read that there are parasites that start off as one creature in the human body, and then evolve as they pass from organ to organ or from host to host. Some parasites can communicate with others, letting the others know that this is a good host to live in. These parasites are in the brain, and they are blocked by heavy drug use…get it?"

"Yes, I get it. That's brilliant. I think you should win the Nobel Prize for that insight," Vato said. He really could not give a shit. I gave up.

We got to the northernmost part of Beach Road. There was a barricade across the street made of piles of tires and sharpened sticks. Judging by the amount of blood on the ground, the area had been overrun.

"Honey, where we go now?" Nok said, as she stopped the rice plow.

"Looks like we're going the rest of the way by foot," I said.

"Arai na?"

"We walk now."

The sun was beginning to set over the ocean. By Thai standards, Pattaya Beach was a cesspool. In the travel brochures, it looked nice – but the reality was far more wretched. Freelance hookers plied their trade along the beach at night, leaving used condoms, cigarette butts, and the occasional syringe, which waited like traps for your feet in the sand. The road was teeming with afflicted, so we decided to walk along the beach. Worst-case scenario: If the horde swarmed us, we could swim into the ocean. There were too many of them for us to take on with a couple of machetes.

On the sand, we spotted a couple of Jet Skis. One still had a key inside. The vehicle was designed for two, but Nok was small and, in the Thai tradition of cramming four people, a baby, and possibly a pet monkey on a scooter, we pulled the Jet Ski into the water and got aboard.

In the distance, we could hear the staccato of gunfire. I drove the Jet Ski parallel to the beach about a hundred yards off the coast. As we neared the entrance to walking street, I saw a massive horde of afflicted in front of a fortified position. Someone with military training had devised the barricade, which was improvised from large tour buses and huge piles of tires that formed watchtowers. Sentries stood guard on the towers, and a machine gun squad was positioned on top of the buses. The horde itself counted in the thousands.

I heard the zip of a gunshot go past my ears. I wasn't sure if it was a warning shot or meant to kill. I pulled the throttle on the Jet Ski and we hauled ass farther south and farther into the ocean. After passing the entrance to Walking Street, we were parallel with the seaside bars and restaurants that lined the coast. Most of the bars along the coast had outdoor sections where you could sit and look over a rail at the fish that gathered to feed on scraps of food. I saw that the open railings had been boarded up or covered with even more tires. In the world of field expedient improvised barriers, tires were the new black.

Another gunshot rang out. I could tell the shooter was in front of us because of the sonic boom the round made when it went past my head. Or so said the movies I had seen. It was obvious that whoever was taking aim at us had a high-powered scope. I raised my hands in the universal sign of *please don't fucking shoot me*.

"What's up with these douchebags, man?" Vato said.

"I have no idea. Don't these retards know the afflicted can't drive motorized personal watercraft?" I said.

"Honey, look. There another boat come," said Nok. She was sandwiched between Vato and me. Vato was wearing the backpack full of drugs and kept freaking out that it would fall off into the ocean.

From the South, a speedboat appeared – coming from the direction of Jomtien. At this point, I felt resigned to my fate. As the boat drew nearer, I heard words called out to us from a bullhorn. They were spoken in a Russian accent.

"Maybe it's those Groped by Gorbachev guys," Vato said.

The boat pulled to within fifty yards. The four guys onboard looked like Chechen rebels. They were decked out in camouflage and ski mask, and each sported a Kalishnakov. I chuckled, as did Vato. Under ordinary circumstances, Guys like this would intimidate me, but I think we were way beyond giving a shit.

A rotund Chechen rebel held the bullhorn and shouted into it for us to follow him. The Chechen boat then turned around and headed towards the seaside end of Walking Street.

"Take off or follow him?" I asked my passengers.

"Just go, man. Get it over with. They probably just want to make sure we aren't infected," Vato said.

"What do you think, baby?" I asked Nok

"Arai gordai," she said

"Huh?" said Vato

"She says it's up to me."

Pulling back on the throttle, I followed the boat to the end of Walking Street, where we found a makeshift dock with a dozen or so more guys dressed like the Chechens. One pulled off his ski mask and revealed the weather-beaten and bearded face of a man from the Caucasus Mountains. Thailand, in recent years had become a haven for everyone from Somali pirates to FARC guerillas, Nigerian scam artists, and the Russian mob. Thailand was the new Casablanca, sheltering people who'd been vomited out of Russian gulags and the darkest African torture rooms. Mercenaries, liars, thieves, spies, and smugglers all desired Thailand's beaches as their personal retirement locale.

A Russian, vodka-eyed and brutish-looking, stepped forward.

"Ah, everything A-okay. You comes to my city and you must checks out with doctor. He say everything A-okay and you can do's some business here. My name Val, and who's is yours?"

"I'm Joel, and this is Nok and Vato," I said.

"Pleasures is mine. Won't you please disembarks from the watercrafts?" Val said.

We got off the Jet Ski, which one of the Chechens plopped his body onto. The rest began smoking ice, passing around the pipe.

"Thank you for bringing backs my watercrafts. Somebody takes it before and they gets eaten by these dead worm heads," Val said. He seemed affable enough.

"Now I takes you to doctor and he looks you over. That A-okay with you guys?" Val asked.

I nodded.

We followed Val to a storefront Thai massage place that had been turned into an impromptu medical center. Men from the front lines, which I gathered was only a few blocks north of us, were getting treated for their wounds.

"I gathers you guys did many copious amounts of drugs ifs you guys alives this long. Only peoples who's seems survives this epidemic are ones who's getting fucked up. I am correct in these thinkings?" Val said. His accent was thick, but nonetheless awesome. I tried to duplicate it so he could better understand us.

"Val, thank you for lettings us into these last bastion of civilization in these worlds full of worm heads. Yes, you are correct in these thinking's you haves of us. We were indeed getting fucked up. My wife Nok has bites on arms from monkey creatures. If doctor can tends her wounds, we gladly pays you in copious amount of drugs," I said.

Vato gave me a look that said both *shut the fuck up* and I'm *going to kill you later.*

"You's guys have copious drugs?" Val asked.

"Not's copious Val. I misspoke," I said. Then I pulled out the baggie of H that Vato had given me. It had at least three or four grams left in it.

"Where's you gets these?" Val asked.

I stammered. My usual capacity for making up on-the-spot bullshit had failed me. Vato came to the rescue as the super Mexican.

"We're here to see the big boss named Chang, and I know you ain't him. So why don't you quit fucking around, Val, and take us to him?" Vato said. He was throwing it down.

"How's you knows Chang?" Val asked.

"I'm his courier. He's expecting me, and I know he doesn't like to be kept waiting."

Val looked Vato up and down. Vato had rolled up his shirt-sleeves to reveal some of his prison ink. A large Virgin De Guadalupe tattoo adorned his forearm. The rest were spider webs and chicks with big titties wearing sombreros. The Virgin herself would have been proud.

Val pulled out his radio and spoke Russian to someone. They went back and forth as Val gripped his AK-47 a little tighter. After several minutes, Val slung the AK over his shoulder and motioned us to follow him.

"Guy is some low-level thug and he's trying to shake down the new fish. It's prison rules dawg, you can't be a bitch with these mofo's," Vato said. He was being extra gangsta.

Val led us outside and down the road to a small side street known as a soi. The bar business was alive and well – the beer bars crammed full of American Marines and sailors who were easy to spot for their boisterous behavior and cranking of speed metal. It was a complete sausage party. By comparison, the British were much more subdued. One bar full of Brits was playing The Spice Girls.

"That's seriously gay," Vato said.

The Russians tended to stay to themselves – frequenting bars that blasted Russian folk music and disco beats from the seventies. We passed a bar catering to Africans, a few of whom sat at the outside tables cutting up lines of cocaine with gunpowder, a mixture called brown-brown.

"I'm expecting the *Star Wars* cantina song to start any minute now," I said to Vato.

Val led us to a bar with smoked-glass windows. More guards of the Chechen variety stood as sentries outside. They patted us down and demanded to look inside Vato's bag. He was having none of it, even when they pointed their guns at him. One of the guards called inside on his radio and exchanged some words in Russian. Static sounded on the guard's radio and then they stepped aside to let us in.

"Haves a good times," one of the Chechens said.

"Spasibo," I replied, meaning "thank you" in Russian. This elicited a Russian bear-style pat on the back, which popped a few of my vertebrae out of alignment.

The inside of the club was opium den chic. It was decorated with brocade curtains, velvet couches, and a contingent of heavily tranquilized leopards chained to a wall. Half-naked women gyrated to a mesmerizing ambient trance soundtrack, while partygoers sitting in booths smoked, shot, or snorted every drug on the DEA no-no list.

"So which one is Genghis Khan?" I asked Vato.

I scanned the crowd, half expecting my eyes to meet a man on a throne getting handfed grapes by slave girls and fanned by servants. The man Vato indicated to me was not nearly as impressive.

"That's him," Vato said.

He pointed to a morbidly obese Thai sitting in a booth. The man was weighed down in thick gold chains and sported half a pound of gold rings. He wore a wifebeater, and – judging by his large, womanly nipples poking through – he was kind of chilly.

"Jabba the Hut over there?" I asked.

"What's with you and the *Star Wars* references?"

"You don't like *Star Wars*?"

"No, I'm not twelve."

"So, I guess you have to give up your bag of China huh?"

Vato's face expressed utter dejection. "Yeah man. This is the cost of admission to Pattaya. I'll be happy with just keeping my life. Can you back me up if something goes wrong?"

I looked around the room and did a quick count of men armed with guns. I stopped when I reached twenty. "Yeah, sure, I got your back, mang. Let's go talk to this fat fuck."

"Seriously man, don't make fun of his weight. He's kind of sensitive."

"He's sensitive with a name like Chang, and he's wearing a wife beater with his man boobs hanging out?" I said. Chang means "elephant" in Thai. I suppose the name could refer to his memory or possibly his schlong.

"Just be cool and let me do the talking," Vato said and then looked over my shoulder. "What's wrong with your girl, bro?"

"Huh?"

"Turn around and check out Nok. She's trippin out, homie."

I turned and looked at Nok. She was standing behind a lady in a booth and picking through the woman's hair. Every time she touched the woman, the woman slapped her hands away. After the rebuff, Nok went right back to doing it again. The woman was Russian, and if she hadn't been extremely fucked up, I'm sure a catfight would have erupted. I rushed over to Nok and pulled her away.

"Babe, what are you doing?" I asked her.

"Oi, I very hungry and I see bug in lady hair and I want to eat," she said.

"Homie, let's do this," Vato called out to me.

"Nok, Just sit down okay? I'll find you some food in a few minutes."

"Okay," she said in a meek voice.

I walked over to Vato again. "Do you have any more of that H in the baggie? I think Nok needs another hit."

Vato dug in his pocket and gave me the baggie, which had only a few grams remaining. "Hurry up, man," he said.

I went back to Nok and handed the baggie to her. "Honey, if you start feeling bad again, just take some more of this, okay?"

She nodded and then put her head down on the table. I hoped she would sleep through whatever happened next. I went back to Vato and dusted off his shirt in an attempt to make him presentable.

"You ready to meet your maker?"

"Let's just get this over with," he said

Chang's opulent fatness took up the better part of the booth. An extremely beautiful Tiffany showgirl flanked him on either side. They were dolled up in pageant wear, replete with tiaras and evening gowns. If you saw them on the street, you would never know they'd been born male.

Vato walked up to the booth and handed his backpack to one of the Tiffany showgirls. Chang was talking on his cell phone to someone in Thai. I talked to Vato out of the corner of my mouth, trying to do my best ventriloquist impersonation.

"Dude, the cell phones are working again," I said.

"Shut up man. Worry about it later."

"Cell phones man, cell phones."

"I know. I fucking heard you the first time. Shut up."

Chang clicked off his phone and began stirring a drink with one of his extremely long pinky fingernails, which looked freshly manicured. So did the Tiffany girls, for that matter.

"So tell me, Ramon, how was your trip to Antwerp?" Chang said to Vato.

"It went well, sir. The Mossad said the bagels are covered in cheese, but they are out of lox."

"No lox? Really? Are you sure they didn't just give all the lox to the Burmese?"

"I don't believe so, sir, but it's always a possibility. The Burmese have started up their own bagel factory and are making their own cheese. They need lox to complete the sandwich."

"Yes, they do. Yes, they do. Tell me, Ramon, how is our old friend Canada? Is she still a whore?"

"Yes, sir. Very much so, sir. Canada has been taken into the FBI witness protection program. We believe that Canada has been spotted somewhere in Nebraska, and is possibly with our old friend Sri Lanka," Vato said. I could tell his voice was starting to shake.

"I knew that whore would go to the Americans. Did the Mossad mention anything about a bagel factory operation in Laos?" Chang said.

"Sir, I can give you a full debrief in written form, if you like."

Chang pulled his fingernail out of the drink and placed a drop of alcohol on his tongue. The movement seemed reptilian. "No, you will debrief me now."

Vato, AKA Ramon, searched for the right words within the lexicon of crimespeak. "The Mossad said to wait for your order, and that if you keep nagging the waitress, she may spit in your food."

"They said that, did they?"

Vato gulped. "Yes, sir."

"Very well then. How did the operation go at the airport? Did you get the package?"

"It's in the bag, sir."

"All of it?"

Vato stammered, "Well, it may be a little short. I had to use some myself in order to get it back to you."

"I commend your efforts to bring this to me. I have many more errands I need you to run." Chang said. He then reached below the table and pulled out a small gold bar. He tossed it to Vato. "This should complete your compensation. That will be the desired currency from now on. That and what you brought for me today."

Vato weighed the bar in his hand. "Thank you, sir."

"Enjoy your stay in Pattaya. I have a hotel room for you. It has all of the amenities you will like. A person will come to see you tonight and give you the details of your next job. You may leave now. Val will take you to where you will stay." Chang said.

He finished his drink and reached over and put his hand in the lap of one of the Tiffany girls. We took that as our cue that the meeting was adjourned.

"Like butter baby," I said to Vato.

"Shut up. We'll talk outside."

"What in the fuck was all that about with the cream cheese and the Mossad?"

"Seriously, homes, you're getting under my skin – what the hell is your girl doing?" he said.

I looked over at Nok. She was accosting the same woman again by picking through her hair and eating imaginary insects.

"She thinks she's a monkey," I said.

"Let's just get her out of here before we blow the mood," Vato said.

"I'm with you."

I led Nok out the front door, trying to act nonchalant, and turned to Vato to ask him another question. He saw it coming a mile away and shook his head.

"Later. Not now," he said.

Vato told Val to take us to the hotel that Chang had booked for us.

"Yes, you guys going to be A-okay, Chang say he going to puts you up in most majestic hotels in Pattaya. Very elegant places you will be staying. Come with me," said Val.

We were taken to a rickshaw pulled by a man dressed in a conservative 1960s-style white shirt and skinny black tie. He looked like a Mormon.

"These your driver," said Val. "He takes you to hotels. You goings to be A-okay."

"Thanks Val," said Vato. "Do you know if there are any girls available at the hotel?"

"Yes but many have worms in pussies. Worms crawls up your dicks and eats your brains. I stays away if I weres you."

Val made an elaborate gesticulation with his hands that sup-posedly pantomimed the act of intercourse, followed by a worm crawling up a man's penis, and then working its way through the body, to its final resting place in the brain. The quasi-performance art sketch culminated with Val having a seizure and worms exploding out of his eyeballs. When he was finished, he pulled back the charging handle on his AK and walked away.

PART II

Our rickshaw started to travel down Walking Street to our hotel. When we sat down, there was a whip inside the rickshaw. I assumed it was intended for use on our Mormon coolie. As tempting as it was, I decided to refrain.

"You can whip me if you like," said the Mormon coolie. "It's how I repent to Jesus for having sinned with my penis."

"Isn't that more of an Opus Dei thing?" I asked him.

"It's *my* thing," he said. "I must do a penis penance."

"Fuck it, just whip him already." Vato said.

"You sure buddy? You won't hold it against me?" I asked the coolie.

"*Please* do it, sir."

"Well, since you said please."

I swung the whip over my head and brought it down on the Mormon coolie's back. I didn't have the technique down, so the whip fell like a wet noodle across his body.

"You have to create a snap through the wrist, dude, so it will travel down the length of the whip," Vato said.

I dropped the whip to the floor of the rickshaw. "Sorry, man, I'm tired. We'll have to give you a penis penance tomorrow."

"Thank you, sir, I must find away to make amends for my transgressions."

"Yo, homie, what drugs were you doing when the shit jumped off?" Vato said.

"You mean when the Angels came?" The coolie said.

"I thought they were parasites," I said

"No, no, no. Not parasites. They are messengers of the Lord. That's why this has only happened in Thailand. This is a place of wickedness and debauchery. The Lord is smiting all the sinners."

"Really? Last time I checked, the only people still alive were the ones getting fucked up on drugs and banging everything in sight," Vato said.

"That is because you are the devil's children. The Lord took the good ones to Heaven with him and left the sinners to live here in the absence of His divine love. The fire of hell is simply the light of God as experienced by those that reject him."

"Wow, you're really a buzzkill, aren't you, man?" I said.

"He's probably a Chester," Vato said.

"What is a Chester, sir?" asked the coolie.

"You know, a booty bandit. You like little kids, don't you?"

"No, sir. My sins are far more wicked. My sins have banned me from Heaven forever."

The coolie walked the rickshaw up to the front of a hotel and stopped.

"Here you are. The Angkor Golden Boner. Enjoy your stay, sir," he said.

We got out of the rickshaw and stood in front of the hotel. The Angkor Golden Boner was a short-time love hotel. I wasn't sure if the owners were Thai or Cambodian. Could have even been a Brit with a sense of humor. When it was named something else, I had seen this hotel before. Then I remembered why it was famous. An expat from the States had chained over a dozen women to the walls in his room. He had removed their teeth and tortured them for months. He'd tried to make them conceive his children. When they didn't get pregnant, he cut up one of the girls and force-fed the pureed remains to the others. He raped and tortured them daily until one of the girls broke free and ran for help. The man fled the country and was never caught. Less than three months later, a Thai horror movie came out depicting the events.

"Damn, dawg, this place is a dump," Vato said.

"It's from that movie about the dude who chained up all those chicks and put them in a blender," I said.

"Arai na?" Nok said. She was starting to look sick again. I couldn't tell her about the history of the hotel. As superstitious as she was, I knew she would never stay here.

"Nothing, babe. How you feel?"

"Oi, have big big buat hua," she said.

"Okay, let's go upstairs, and I'll get you something for your headache. Then you can lay down, okay?"

She nodded as if it took her last bit of energy. I'd once spent twelve hours on a bus ride with her, and she hadn't said a word the whole time. It was one of the things I liked about her. When she was quiet for long periods, it didn't mean something was wrong, it just meant she knew when to leave a brother alone.

"I just hope I'm not sleeping in a puddle of cum. This place looks gnarly," Vato said.

We checked into the hotel, and I was amused to learn that the concierge actually wanted to photocopy our passports. The guy behind the counter probably hadn't been paid for a month or more, but still held out hope that things would return to normal and feared that the big boss would yell at him for not doing his job – even at the end of the world.

They gave us one room with a double bed.

"Maybe they think we're having a three-way," Vato said.

"Just hope they have hot showers," I said.

"Should be a nice surprise in the room for us. There is every time Chang puts me up in a hotel."

"He always puts you up in a shithole like this?" I said.

"He prefers the term 'safehouse,' I think."

The elevators didn't work, so we had to walk up six flights to our room. In Cambodia, rents were cheaper on the lower levels for this very reason. I realized why the hotel was called Angkor.

The room's interior was mindboggling, even by love-hotel standards. Heart-shaped beds and bathtub. Love swing over the bed. Mirrors everywhere. When I caught my reflection, I caught a flash of something moving in the corner of my eye. All around us were the creatures I'd seen when I'd worn the toupee. To see them, I only needed to adjust my eyes.

Vato began to look around the room for something. He opened all the drawers and finally found it in an antique Chinese armoire.

"That armoire is a little out of place, don't you think?" I said.

"Not really, man. You can pick up antiques in Asia for next to nothing. People all think that the ghosts of whoever owned it are drawn to their furniture and shit. Having this in a Thai person's house is almost as bad as summoning a demon."

"So what's inside?"

"Check it out, yo," Vato said, and pulled out an antique opium tray with all the original equipment. It had an oil lamp, long needles to spin the opium, and a beautiful pipe with a door-knob-shaped bowl I figured would be worth a shitload on EBay.

We each took a hot shower, and I put Nok to bed after giving her some H. Vato and I sat on the floor while he fired up the oil lamp. A porcelain urn held a golf-ball-sized chunk of opium. From a few feet away, I could detect its floral aroma.

Vato placed an opium pellet in the pipe and held it over the lamp.

"When I was young and living in Cali, I parked my car in the garage and was about to turn it off and go inside the house. I was sitting in the car and listening to a radio show. The car exhaust started filling the garage, and I began to feel drowsy. I knew what was happening to my body, and I knew if I left the engine on that I would go to sleep and never wake up. I wasn't depressed. I didn't hate my life. I don't know what it was but something just made me want to leave the engine on and see what happened. I started to get a headache and feel nauseated. My eyelids grew heavy, and I started to close them. The headlights were on in the car, and the windows were fogging up. I saw something through the windshield. A shape of some kind. It was a human form standing in front of my car. The lights were on but I couldn't see who it was through the car exhaust and the fog on the windows. The shape started to move from side to side, as if gently dancing and rolling its hips. Then the shape stretched out a pair of long, slender arms and placed them on the hood. It moved gracefully like a woman, and began to climb onto the front of my car. I still couldn't see it clearly. It was as if it was made of shadow. It crawled towards the windshield and placed its hands on the glass. I was almost out by now. My eyes were closing and my mind was completely clouded by the fumes. I opened them one last time and saw a face staring at me through the glass. It was a woman. Her face was beautiful with a subtle hint of malice. She had big, catlike eyes, and full lips. She smiled at me. Her teeth were perfect and white. She opened her mouth, and her head began to convulse. Her head came through the windshield. It didn't break through, dawg – it *came* through. Her mouth widened and I was looking down into a cave. What I saw down there..."

Vato took a long pull from the opium pipe. He held the smoke in his lungs and exhaled a blue plume of vapor.

"What I saw down there could only be described as a perfect mixture of paradise and some kind of hell realm. I saw beautiful, white sand beaches with crystal clear water and piles of burning bodies. I saw myself on a bed, boning a group of beautiful women. Our twisted bodies and limbs morphed into something out of a fucking Bosch painting. It was if I were standing in front of a door. I had the choice to enter or not. Nothing was forced upon me. I was seeing another world. My next life. Or maybe the possibilities within this life. Then I felt hands pulling me out of my car. I woke up in a hospital. The rest is…well, I'm here, right? After I got out of the hospital, I knew my purpose. I had to see the world. I never stopped to reflect on who that woman was in the garage that night. Maybe it was an angel, or a demon. Who the fuck knows? Whatever she was, she showed me the possibilities in this lifetime."

Vato let the opium pipe fall from his hand.

"Everything I've seen so far; things I can never tell anyone about, have led me to one conclusion – that there are no gods… just a world like ours, only full of spirits. They have their leaders, too. Some are elected. Some appointed. Some who took power by force. They have a beginning as well – an evolution. They evolved the same way we did. They wage war and have their criminals and madmen. In their world, they call no one God. It's the same as in prison, dawg. There are shot-callers and bitches…and guess what? Now they're here."

There was a knock at the door.

"Can you get that, homes?" Vato said. The urban gangster slang was obviously part of his act or his cover. I didn't know what to believe, but somehow I trusted him. I opened the door and one of the Chechens was there. He handed me a manila envelope and left without saying a word.

"I suppose this is for you," I said and held it out to Vato.

"You open it, dawg. Whatever happens, you're in this with me now. I'll cut you in on whatever I get paid, which is usually a lot," he said.

I opened up the envelope, half expecting it to explode, or, at the very least, for Anthrax powder to spill out. What I saw made me shout – "Holy titty fucking Christ!"

"What is it, dawg?"

I held up the pictures. One was a telephoto lens shot of a man who was dressed like a woman and carrying an Igloo cooler. The other was a close-up of a terrible-looking hairpiece.

****

"His name is Yuri, it says. He's former CIA, and now he's working freelance for private intelligence contractors," I said, reading the dossier that accompanied the photos.

"Who the fuck would hire that freak?" Vato said. "He's a walking basket case."

"Apparently, he's really good at his job. Maybe good help is hard to find these days."

"What else does it say about him?"

"Not a lot. Apparently, he's been watching the watchers, because he's been spying on your boss's whole operation," I said.

"Dressed in drag and walking around with severed body parts in an Igloo cooler?"

"Yep, that's what it looks like."

"So what the fuck do they want us for? He's dead, ain't he?"

"I guess not. It says we are to retrieve the KH-32 reconnaissance hairpiece."

"The Donald Trump toupee?"

"I told you I was seeing shit when I wore it. It nearly drove me nuts. I'm still seeing shit out of the corner of my eyes. It's like a bad trip."

"K-what's it called?"

I checked the dossier again, "KH-32 reconnaissance hairpiece."

"A recon hairpiece?"

"Dude, read it yourself," I said and handed Vato the dossier.

Vato scanned the paper and looked at the photos. That *what the fuck?* Look I had come to know was back again. "So, you think he was following us? He couldn't have just met us on the street by accident. Nothing is that random."

"I have no fucking idea, man. You're the one with the Mossad contacts and whatnot."

Vato read the dossier several times. He chortled. "It says they want us to retrieve the Donald Trump recon hair hat thingy. Do you remember where we were when I threw it out of the tuk-tuk?"

I shrugged.

"Fuck. We had it in our hands," Vato said.

"What happens if you don't take the gig?"

"Banishment or maybe something not so nice."

A note slid under the door. There were several other things that happened in the room that coincided with our conversation. When I bitched about there being no toilet paper, the front desk guy appeared with several rolls. We didn't say it aloud, but we knew the room was bugged.

"What's the note say?" Vato asked.

"There's three tickets for Diarrhea Bukakke tonight at the front gate. Wherever that is."

"Probably by the entrance to Walking Street, where we saw those buses and towers made from tires. That's all it says?"

"No, we've gotta go meet Chang again at his bar about an hour before. Show starts at ten, so we gotta be there by nine," I said.

"What time is it now?"

"I don't have a watch. Do you?"

"If I did, I wouldn't have asked you."

The room phone rang. I looked at Vato. It seemed he wasn't getting up off the floor anytime soon.

"Hello?" I said into the phone.

"Yes, hello, sir. Now it five in nighttime. You want I wake you at eight in nighttime?" said the voice of the front desk guy.

I scanned the room. With all of the love contraptions and tacky decorations, a bug could be planted anywhere.

"That will be fine. Thank you."

"Will there be anything else you may need, sir?"

"You need anything, dude?" I asked Vato.

"Yeah, I want a girl from the hotel bar to come up here."

"What about the worms, man?"

"Sorry, sir, only lady we have is lady who make milk with her boob," the front desk dude said.

"Guy says they only have a girl who is lactating," I relayed.

"Well, like the old saying goes, "When life gives you a lactating woman, sometimes you gotta make cheese.' I'll take her," Vato said.

"What? You gonna bang her in here?" I said.

"No, man. I'm gonna take bath in one of those goofy-looking tubs and have her give me a soapy."

"Sorry, sir, water in tub don't work," the front desk guy said.

"Tub doesn't work, dude," I said.

"Send her up anyway."

"You should sleep, man. We've only got three hours before we gotta wake up again," I told Vato.

"You go lay down with Nok. I'll crash on the floor with cheese tits. This homie needs love, too, you know."

"Okay, send her up," I told the front desk dude.

I moved onto the bed next to Nok and put my arm around her waist. Her skin felt warm, and her hair smelled like cheap shampoo. Her breath was labored, and her face was scrunched up in scowl of pain. I looked at the bite marks on her arm. The suppurating wounds didn't seem to be healing at all. Small black bumps appeared under the skin around the bite, and, as I looked closer, I saw one move. I held my head back from her and looked at her body.

Again, the shadows and figures were just out of my peripheral vision. At the foot of the bed, I could see a small childlike apparition playing peek-a-boo with me. I ignored it and focused my gaze on Nok. Whatever residual otherworldly vision the KH-32 recon hairpiece had imparted to me, I could now see details in this world I had never seen before. I looked at Nok's back and could see through her clothes and under her skin. I saw her heart beating and her blood flowing through her veins.

Then I saw them crawling through her body. They appeared as black lines or as a cancerous mass would show up on an x-ray. They wound around her spine and up into her head. At the base of her skull, I saw a nest of them curling around her brain stem. More burrowed through her fat and muscles. Others appeared to fight or mate, I couldn't tell which. My gaze went to her stomach. I saw something in her abdomen. Something smaller even than the worms. It had arms and legs, hands and feet, and the unmistakable outline of a human head. The worms hadn't wound around it yet. The fetus floated in embryonic fluid, sleeping and waiting for its chance to be born.

I couldn't process what I was seeing. The exhaustion of the day's events, coupled with the drugs, and the little shit ghost that was still fucking with me at the foot of the bed made it hard to think. When I saw the shadow reappear by my feet, I kicked it in the face. The room shook for a few seconds and the air got colder. The hair stood up on the back of my neck and I felt an icy wind behind my ear.

"Fuck off!" I yelled.

"Sup, man? You okay?" Vato asked.

"Just dandy."

There was a knock at the door.

"That's probably cheese tits. You get it," I said.

Vato pushed the opium tray to the corner of the room and went to the door.

"What's up, mama? Oh, goddamn those titties are huge. Dude, you gotta see this chick," Vato said.

His voice sounded as if he was underwater or I was. That was when I fell asleep – which was also when the nightmares began

****

I was falling off the edge of a cliff, down to ocean waves breaking on rocks. As my arms flailed, I saw flashes of all of my previous incarnations. When most people talk about their past life regressions, they tend to envision themselves as someone special such as Napoleon or a Roman emperor. Not me – at least not in this dream or nightmare. I saw how truly insignificant I'd been in every one of my lifetimes. I saw myself as a caveman, living in the forest and with insects eating me alive. My body was disease-ravaged and my teeth were rotting and painful. Life was short, life was shitty, and thankfully it was soon over. In another flash, I saw myself as a guy with an extremely ugly nose, who had committed suicide over a woman. In yet another, I was a terrible poet, who was the laughingstock of an entire nation and era – yep, committed suicide by hanging. It got to the point as I was falling and watching my lives and deaths that I got to thinking – do I ever not fucking kill myself in one of these things? Just as that thought entered my head and as the waves and rocks were just about to make me go splat, I saw people holding me on their shoulders and a crowd lauding me as a hero. Women threw themselves at my feet and asked me to autograph their tits. Others simply promised their undying love. I had no idea what I was famous for, but it made me smile in my sleep – and, just like every other time that I'd had a good dream, something totally fucked up happened and woke me up.

It was the sounds of choking. I thought maybe I was strangling Nok in her sleep, but my hands were over her breasts – not her throat. The sound was coming from the floor. I sat up and saw Vato with his head buried in cheese tits' crotch with what appeared to be a giant squid coming out of her pussy. It had its tentacles locked around his face, and the woman was holding down his head with her hands. It appeared as though she was trying to swallow him with her vajayjay.

"Yo, what the fuck?" was all I could think to say.

After I jumped out of bed, I tripped over a power cord that hadn't been there before. (I knew my stumble was the Phii Dek paying me back for kicking it in the face). I fell on the floor and a light bulb unscrewed itself from an overhead lamp, landed on my head, and exploded into shards. When I stood up and tried to hop over to Vato, I stepped in the glass shards, which cut the shit out of my feet.

"Okay, I'm fucking sorry already. Sheesh," I apologized to the Phii Dek for kicking it in the face. I also asked it to help me extract Vato's head from the vajayjay monster, and if the ghost child complied, I promised to buy him a toy.

"Mmmmmfffff," Vato said.

I reached down to lift up Vato's feet up and pull him away from cheese tits. In her eyes, she had the look of the possessed. My eyes panned down to her gargantuan rack. Vato wasn't lying – her titties were huge. Just then, cheese tits let go of Vato's head and squeezed her breasts.

A double barrel shotgun blast of rancid milk shot out of her nipples and pinned me against the wall. There seemed to be no end to the stream of milky puss. She raised a titty and aimed it at my mouth. It had the force of a pressure washer or a fire hose. My mouth filled with one stream of titty milk while the other kept my torso pinned to the wall. I could hear Vato struggling for air above my own sounds of gurgling. I spoke to the Phii Dek with my mind. *"Okay, I'll buy you two toys,"* I said.

"No, I want five," was his counter offer

"How about three?" I haggled

"Four," the Phii Dek said.

"Okay, four."

We agreed, and then he added, *"If you forget to buy them for me, I will never ever stop fucking with you."*

"Deal."

The antique Chinese armoire started to rock back and forth, until it fell over with a crash and landed on cheese tits' head. Her spray of milk stopped and I vomited out what seemed to be a gallon of the stuff. Cheese tits was pinned under the armoire but still alive. Her arms flailed and she tried to lift the armoire from her head. I reached down and snatched up Vato's' legs. As I pulled, cheese tits' pelvis made a cracking sound and her hips dislocated. It was like watching a Burmese python unhinge its own jaw so it could swallow larger prey.

As hard as I could, I yanked on Vato's legs but he didn't budge. But I then felt an unseen hand grab his legs and pull with an amazing amount of force. When Vato's head popped out of cheese tits' vajayjay, it sounded like the opening of a champagne bottle.

What followed could only be described as the biggest queef of all time.

"You okay, dude?" I asked Vato. He seemed stunned – and rightly so.

"That was really awful. I mean just really, really awful, man," he said, spitting little bits of residue out of his mouth.

Cheese tits was struggling under the weight of the armoire, and she began firing random blasts of milk around the room in a vain attempt to hit one of us.

"Hang on, dude," Vato said. He then jumped on top of the armoire and started stomping on it. "Yo, help me out, homie," he said.

I hopped up on top of the armoire, and we began to jump up and down in unison until we heard a squishy, crunchy sound and the armoire suddenly got lower.

"Hey, mang, is Nok okay? She's not a sleeper is she? Cuz that girl is out cold."

I felt an icy hand on my leg and then felt a chilled breeze. I could see the Phii Dek run across the room with that awkward little-kid gait children have. It leapt onto the bed with Nok and cuddled up next to her. It then turned its head towards me and stared through my soul. Its eyes were both loving and vengeful. It had been betrayed before – drowned in a toilet by its previous mother. He patted Nok on the belly and smiled. "*Mamma, mamma,*" he said.

I was kind of fuzzy on the issue of when a fetus becomes imbued with a soul. Up until I wore the toupee, I had never believed in anything. I didn't know if these were really ghosts, or hallucinations, or the worms messing with my mind. The way the Phii Dek looked at me, I knew it was claiming ownership of Nok's pregnancy. Either that or hijacking it.

"What did you say before about gods just being creatures from another world?"

Vato stepped off of the armoire and began packing up the opium kit in his bag.

"I dunno, man. Whatever I said before, forget I said it."

"You said something about them waging wars, and being shot callers and bitches."

"I said that?"

"Yeah, man. Please elaborate."

"What time is it? Don't we gotta go to that punk show?" Vato said.

The phone rang.

"Guess that's our wake-up call," I said.

Vato walked over and answered the phone. "It's dead," he said.

From my vantage point on top of the armoire, I could see the phone cord. It wasn't plugged in. Out of the corners of my eyes, I could see them all around me. They appeared just for a second and were gone. I closed my eyes and opened them. This time, the shadows were closer. I was afraid to blink or they might appear right on top of me. From the corner of my eye, I saw the walls of the room. They were totally moldy and dilapidated. When I looked in front of me, I saw the tacky accoutrements of the love hotel. My eyes were starting to water from not blinking, so I held them open with my fingers.

"Dude, wake up Nok. We gotta get the fuck out of here," I said.

Vato looked up at me and chuckled. "What's with your eyes, homie?"

"Hurry, I'm serious," I said.

I stepped off of the armoire and tripped. When I reached out to regain my balance, I saw them. Even worse, I saw everything.

The room had changed. I looked at the floor, where I saw pools of blood and piles of excrement. To my right, I saw ten women chained to the wall. They were filthy and terror-stricken. Their eyes showed not the fear of death, but the fear of not dying. Their eyes held the fear of what would happen next. I could hear the sounds of an axe dropping and then the sounds of a knife cutting. They were the sounds of a butcher shop or a slaughterhouse. I turned my head, and I saw him. It was the farang who had never been caught. He was placing a captive woman's arm in an old-style meat grinder. He had done all of this in front of the others. The chained women were forced to watch each other raped. They suffered through the screams of the women as they were murdered and the horror of watching them dismembered. The farang took the ground-up meat of the dead women and placed it in dog food bowls. He forced the chained women to eat from the bowls while he violated them in ways I can't describe.

This was that room. Once I awakened to the truth of the place, it no longer had the illusion of a remodeling job. I saw underneath the heart-shaped tubs to the place where the killer had slept. He had arranged the severed body parts from different victims and formed them into some kind of idealized vision of his perfect woman. There was a beautiful woman's head, the torso of another with full breasts, and the legs and arms of others. I looked up at the women chained to the walls, and they knew I could see them. This was even more terrifying than the vision itself. For when the women knew I could see them, their eyes went wild with desperation for me to help. That desperation turned to rage, a rage that filled the room and made the foundation of the hotel shake.

"She won't wake up, man," Vato said.

"Pick her up please," I said.

"She's your girl, bro. You carry her."

The floor was moving, and I had trouble walking the distance to the bed. My vision was now reversed. Instead of seeing the shadow world out of the corner of my eyes, now it was the real world I could only see peripherally.

I put my hands out in front of myself and felt the empty space the way I'd feel my way in the dark.

"I could really use your help, man," I said.

Vato threw on his backpack and heaved Nok onto his shoulder. He led me by the hand out of the room the way a fireman would rescue people from a burning building. In the hallway, apparitions walked by. The hotel pulsated like the beat of a heart blackened by disease. I could see into the other rooms as Vato led us downstairs. Every room I peered into was a glimpse into desperate and lonely lives. This short-time hotel had created endless misery. Many of the souls that wandered its halls and slept in its beds would never leave. Even if this place was burned to the ground, the vortex of pain that it occupied in time and space would live forever – and there wasn't anything I could do but watch.

Vato got us to the ground floor and out onto the street. He transferred Nok to my arms, and we all sat down in front of the hotel. This place of evil would later become a tourist Mecca.

Our fascination with predators and killers is hardwired into our DNA. Understanding the thing that can kill or eat you and turn your life into a nightmare is a gruesome necessity of life. I could tell that the women chained to the wall had been thinking about that new purse they wanted or were preoccupied with unimportant bullshit. They never noticed the shadow looming in the corners. They never heard the footsteps behind them in the dark. Then one day they woke up bleeding from the head and chained to a wall. Now my eyes were opened, and I could see everything I wanted to see. Nothing would ever sneak up on me again.

"So you wanna go and catch that show?" Vato said

"Oi. Where we go?" Nok said, as she woke up.

"We have to go see that guy named Chang again," I said.

I saw the Phii Dek hiding behind a light post. He was trying to start the peek-a-boo game again – and was telling me he wanted his toys *now*.

"I have to find a place that sells kids toys. Like, right away. There's gotta be a market in this town, right?" I said.

"Where's our rickshaw guy?" Vato said.

I looked up and down the street and didn't see him.

"Let's just walk," I said.

Nok whined, "Oi, you say you going to give me food before. Now I don't eat for a long time."

"Okay, baby, we'll get you some food. Just hang on. We have to walk and maybe we will see something along the way," I said, and thought to myself: *this is what parenthood will be like – trying to get something done but it takes forever because you have to stop for ice cream breaks to keep everyone happy.* Now I simply needed to find a toy, no – make that four toys for a ghost baby and papaya salad for a worm-infested pregnant lady.

"There's the rickshaw guy," Vato said pointing down the street.

The Mormon coolie was pulling a load full of ladyboys along with their customers. Unlike us, the customers were having a field day whipping the shit out of the Mormon. He yelped in what sounded like a mixture of pain and ecstasy.

"Why are there so many ladyboys in this town?" Vato asked. "They're like pigeons."

"Yeah, I'll bet you every one of those guys is gonna get eaten by a ladyboy ass monster tonight," I said.

In fact, I knew it. I could see one of the ladyboys had a large amount of barbed worms in her balls, and another had row after row of shark like teeth lining her anus. Since they weren't going crazy, that meant they were all on drugs. The drugs simply masked the symptoms. Whatever these parasites were, they were causing the whole human body to evolve into a monster.

The rickshaw pulled up to our hotel and the ladyboys and their customers climbed out. The customers were all heavily armed with TAR-21 assault rifles. It was the standard infantry rifle for the Thai army after it phased out the M16. These guys had high and tight haircuts, and, judging by their accents, I figured they were Marines.

"Move it, fuck stick," one of them said to me as he passed. He was the guy paired up with shark-teeth anus girl.

So much for giving him a warning, I thought.

We climbed into the rickshaw and told the Mormon coolie to take us back to Chang's bar. I also told him to stop if he saw any papaya salad or kids' toys for sale. The back of the Mormon coolie's shirt was ripped open and blood ran down his body from the whiplashes. I couldn't see any traces of the worms within his body. As far as I could tell, he was in perfect health.

As we rode, I looked over at Nok and I jumped a little. The Phii Dek was lying in her lap and suckling from one of her nipples. He took his mouth off of her breast for a second and winked at me. "*Mamma*," he said, and then gave me a thumbs up.

I made a mental note to buy him really cheap toys with sharp edges and lots of lead paint in them.

When the Mormon coolie spoke, he sounded rather morose. He told us about his Sisyphean task of carting hookers around all night with their customers, and, as of yet, hadn't received a really spectacular penis penance.

"There is a woman selling children's toys up ahead. Would you like me to stop?" the Mormon coolie asked.

I looked down at the Phii Dek in Nok's lap. He glared at me and flashed a smile full of piranha teeth. Then he opened his mouth nice and wide and acted as if he were going to bite off the end of Nok's breast.

"Yes, stop please," I said.

"Oi, why we stop? I'm hungry!" Nok said.

"Oi, because we have to buy a bunch of freaking toys for the ghost baby in your lap who is about to bite your titty off," I said.

"Arai na?" she said.

"Never mind. Just hang on a second."

I hopped out of the rickshaw and walked up to a table where a toothless old lady who reeked of urine sold kids' toys.

"Hurry, homes," Vato called out to me.

Without looking at him, I flipped him off over my shoulder.

"Okay, what do you want, you little fucker?" I mentally projected to the Phii Dek.

The Phii Dek looked over the assortment of toys laid out on the table. For the most part, the selection consisted of small cars and big plastic trucks. There was also an array of counterfeit Yu-Gi-Oh! cards and annoying-sounding plastic ray guns. The Phii Dek pointed at a pink horse with a flowing blonde mane, a knock off Barbie doll, a Dora hairbrush, and a Justin Timberlake coloring book with crayons.

"Wow, that's super gay." I said to him with my mind.

"They are not for me," the Phii Dek said. *"They are for a friend of mine. She is a little girl who die same as me. She have nobody to buy her toys."*

"You don't want anything for yourself?" I asked.

"No, because we say you buy me four toys, and I just want you to buy for my friend," he said. *"Nobody love her, and I am her only friend."*

"Oh, my god, that's so sad," I thought. *"This could be on an episode of Oprah, and millions of viewers would sob into their vagi-wipes."*

To reward his generosity toward his friend, I was about to buy a few toys for him, then realized this was Thailand – and even the ghosts were scam artists.

"Okay, well, tough shit then. A deal's a deal," I told him.

I paid the toothless urine lady, and she put the toys in a plastic grocery bag. I held out my arm for the Phii Dek to take the bag.

"I'm dead, you idiot," he said. *"Put them over there on the ground so I can play with my friend."*

"You don't seem to have a hard time knocking furniture over, but you can't carry a plastic bag? What's up with that?" I said.

"That takes a lot of energy. It makes me weak. I only do it so we can have toys."

I walked over to the spot the Phii Dek had indicated and set down the bag of toys.

"No, you fucking dipshit. Take them out of the bag and arrange them on the ground. We are dead, you retard," the Phii Dek said.

"That's a nice mouth on you for a little kid. Where'd you learn to talk that way?"

"I use the words from within your mind. These are your words. I can speak to someone in any language. Your mind is full of filth and obscenity," he said.

He was right, and there was no sense in arguing with him. I took the toys out of the plastic bag and placed them on the ground. I even took the crayons out of the box and opened up the coloring book to a picture of Justin Timberlake thrusting his pelvis in the air. From behind a food vendor's cart, came a little girl no more than four years old. She was adorable in every sense – like dolphins dipped in sunshine and wrapped in rainbows. She was shy and didn't seem to want to come near me. The Phii Dek took her by the hand and told her to sit down.

"Okay, have fun kids," I said.

Both of the ghost children put their palms together in a respectful way and bowed to me.

"If you need my help again, just call," said the Phii Dek.

"Yeah? You got a phone?"

"Just close your eyes and quiet your mind. Try to make everything sabai sabai. Then say out loud: I'm a fucking retard, and I need a Thai ghost child to help me out because I am such an incompetent fuckwad. Say that three times and I will come and help you."

I wondered if there were any back-alley abortion clinics in this town. If not, I might just have to throw Nok down a flight of stairs. There was no way I was going to be this kid's dad. I no longer blamed his mom for drowning him in the toilet.

"Of course," I said. *"How many toys do you want next time?"*

"Depends on the task. I think the next one might be rather large."

"What makes you say that?"

The Phii Dek looked at the little girl and they both giggled. When they laughed, their eyes changed to something ancient and sinister. I got the sensation that these beings were over a thousand years old, and were disguising themselves as children for the mere novelty of it.

"When the burned man comes looking for you tonight, don't run from him. He alone can save you all. We will both be there for you in your hour of need," he said.

"Why would you help me? What burned man? Esmeralda the freak?"

The two ghost babies let out that malevolent giggle. The Phii Dek pointed to Nok in the Rickshaw.

"Mamma," he said, and then the two of them disappeared.

I walked back to the rickshaw and got inside. I thought about something and then got back out. I stood in front of the Mormon coolie and smiled.

"For your sins, my son," I said and kicked him squarely in the nuts.

The Mormon coolie began barfing on the street, and I got back in the rickshaw. I picked up the whip and began flogging the shit out of him.

"Thank you, sir," the coolie said.

"Hurry up, we're late," I barked.

"Bro, you okay? You seem a little high-strung," Vato said.

I didn't say anything and just stared ahead as the rickshaw began to move. The street was lit up like a Third World Las Vegas. Walking Street at the end of the world was nothing less than bedlam. On a normal night – when it wasn't the apocalypse – Walking Street was a seedy but fun whorehouse of a city within a city. I knew men who never left the protective magical circle they had drawn around their barstools. Well, they may have walked a few yards to go get food, and another few yards to go sleep, maybe even visit an ATM, but for the most part they got off a plane in Bangkok, took a taxi to Pattaya, and slept, ate, and fucked within a very small bubble. That guy was now the lord of odious vices. The Darwinism of the clean and sober had left the junkies and drunks as the inheritors of the world. I could see into the bodies of those walking around with their assault rifles and knew which ones had worms and which ones had just been infected. I saw one man whose entire internal organ structure had been changed. All that remained of his original make-up were his heart and a gland under his armpit.

At the rate the worms were evolving and the rate at which these men were consuming booze and drugs, it was only a matter of time until the convergence of two forces. Either the drugs would run out and everyone would become afflicted, or the monster growing inside of them would take over, and whatever was left that cared about staying human would be gone.

Guitar feedback, played through giant amplifiers, filled the air, followed by screaming in Thai that sounded like someone getting a gender reassignment surgery without anesthetic. The crowd screamed and people started shooting automatic weapons in the air. Everyone was armed to the max. Even the street food vendors had machetes within easy reach. The stage was situated at the entrance to Walking Street. Behind the stage was the rear of the castle-like fortress made from tires and abandoned buses. A thump thump thump began as the double bass drum from the on-stage band fired up.

"That must be the opening act," Vato said.

The stage lights flared up to reveal a group of absolutely hideous and unpassable ladyboys. The lead singer was about six feet four inches tall and had an Adam's apple the size of a hand grenade. She wore a leather dominatrix getup with fuck-me boots, and had a handgun strapped to her thigh. She "sang" through a pitch shifter and acted like a composite of every bad NYC underground punk rock singer from the eighties. Before the first song came to an end, she had pissed into the audience, shit on the stage, and cut her arms with a razor. When the worms popped out of her wounds, she either ate them or hurled the creatures into the audience.

"Yeah, whatever. GG Allin did that ages ago," I said.

The first song didn't really end, but melded into a cover of Los Angeles by X. We arrived at the front of Chang's bar and the Mormon coolie let us out. Val was outside.

"Welcomes back. You enjoys your stays at hotels?" he said.

"Marvelous. Is Chang inside?" Vato said.

"Yes, yes. Enter, please," Val said and opened the door.

I could hear the crowd explode into a cheer for whatever was happening on stage. I looked up and saw the lead singer doing things to a dead body. I turned my head before I was burdened with one more image I didn't want burned into my memory.

The inside of the club looked as if it were hosting Caligula's birthday party. Chechen rebels replaced the Praetorian Guard, and instead of a woman playing a cithara, there was a sad Chinese crooner singing mournful renditions of ABBA hits. We walked in as he was churning out the lyrics to "Dancing Queen" with all the enthusiasm of a leaking faucet.

On the dance floor was a live sex show that featured people who had undergone an almost-complete transformation by the worms.. Ribcages opened up and the ribs became skeletal arms that pulled the lover on top until something within sucked out its juices. One man sat naked and terrified in a chair while a group of monstrous-looking katoeys stood around him and bukakkied on his face. Instead of semen, the katoeys shot out black worms, which proceeded to devour the man's head. He screamed in pain as they burrowed into his eyes and crawled up his nose.

It turned out that the man in the chair had failed on one of Chang's errands. A Chechen told me this as I stood staring slack-jawed at the show. This was the petty caprice of every despot that had suddenly awakened to his power. Everyone from Tiberius to Uday Hussein had fallen under its spell. Chang's penchant for horror mixed with sexuality would have made Vlad the Impaler blush.

From across the room, Chang motioned us toward him. I turned to look for Nok but she was gone. After searching the room for her, I spotted her at the buffet table stuffing her face.

"Just leave her," Vato said. "She only seems happy when she's sleeping or eating."

"Yep, she's Just like every other Thai girl. What do you think Chang is gonna ask us to do? You don't think he's gonna send us out to look for the toupee?" I said.

"I've got an idea. Just play along," Vato said and then crossed to Chang's table.

I followed behind and tried to avoid the dance floor, which was now covered in worms from the bukakke chair incident. At Chang's table were two farang men in suits.

"Happy birthday, sir," Vato said as he approached the table.

"Yes, it's my birthday. Did you bring me my present?" Chang said.

"What present, sir?" Vato asked.

"Didn't you get the photos I sent?'

"With all due respect, sir, that was only a few hours ago. I thought this meeting was about how we were going to get it."

"So you failed me then, did you?" Chang said.

Vato looked at me. I took that as my cue to say something.

"Mister Chang, I think I know the location of the items you are looking for. In fact, we know the person you are looking for. Give us time and we can find both," I said.

"Who are you, if I may ask?" one of the suit men said.

"I'm…Barry," I said.

"Barry, would you like to see something important? Something that may even save the world?" he said.

I shrugged.

The two men in suits spoke into Chang's ears. They then nudged the Tiffany showgirls out of the booth.

"Okay, we show them. Then we come back for my birthday party. Cake going to be very sexy," Chang said and pointed to a back door we were supposed to go through.

As we walked to the back door, the sad Chinese crooner started a slow, melancholy version of Wham!'s "Wake Me Up Before You Go Go." Vato went in through the door first and let out a giant "God-dayam, dawg." I followed, and, while less excited than Vato, I did let a few expletives fly.

The room behind the bar had stacks of gold bars, giant sacks of white powder, bag after bag of weed, and weapons of every kind piled as high as the ceiling. Inside the room, several of the guards were using a hundred-pound sack marked COCAINE in big block letters as a table where they did lines of even more cocaine.

"Willy fucking Wonka, yo," Vato said.

Chang and the guys in suits followed us in and closed the door.

"Do you know what this is, Barry?" suit guy number two asked.

"Uh, yeah," I said.

"How would you describe what you are seeing?"

"It's a big-ass room full of drugs…and gold…and weapons," I said, stating the obvious

"You're wrong on all three counts Barry," the suit guy said. He spoke as if he were narrating a late-night infomercial. "On count number one, you stated that you saw drugs. Where you see drugs, I see medicine. On count number two, you are also in error. For where you see gold, I see operational funding. On count number three, however, you are only half wrong. These are not weapons in the sense that they are used to kill. Rather, these are tools for the implementation of law and order. So you see, Barry, it's a simple matter of paradigm shift. Wouldn't you agree?"

I looked around the room. I could tell that each guard snorting blow from the table made from blow was about two days away from having his esophagus detach itself from his neck and strangle his comrades while they slept. I could also tell that Chang's swollen-girl nipples that poked through his wife beater were about to start poking out even more. For, behind a giant stack of gold bricks, I saw the Phii Dek and his little girl pal. They were playing their usual game with me, and, as soon as I saw them, the temperature in the room got cold.

"Yeah, same same but different," I said. I didn't see any difference – or care, for that matter.

"I beg to differ Barry," the suit guy said. "It's not the same, and it is quite, quite different."

The other suit guy chimed in. "When were you last in contact with the KH-32 reconnaissance hairpiece?"

"We saw it this afternoon. At the time, it was worn by that guy you're looking for, only he called himself Esmeralda, not Yuri," I said.

"You were in contact with Yuri?"

Vato knew these people better than I did. I didn't know what I should or shouldn't say, so I let him do the talking.

"Yeah, we saw him up in Bangkok. He was a survivor, and he was wearing that thing you guys are looking for," Vato said.

The men in the suits looked nonplused. "You mean he was wearing it on his head and walking around the city with it?" number two asked.

"Yep."

"How would you describe his demeanor?"

"Demeanor…Hmmm." Vato turned to me. "Barry, how would you describe Esmeralda?"

I let them have it. The whole episode. Everything from him wearing the Paris Hilton impersonator's face, to his final demise at the hands of Johnny Walker. The suits, however, only wanted to know about the toupee.

"Where is the KH-32 reconnaissance hairpiece now?"

"It's on the tollway between Pattaya and Bangkok," Vato chimed in. "Homie here, I mean Barry, was wearing it and freaking out so I threw it out of the tuk-tuk we were in. I didn't think it was important. My bad."

Suit guy number one walked up to me and shined a small flashlight in my eyes. He asked me to follow his finger with my eyes, to stand on one leg, and other shit, in what amounted to a field sobriety test.

"How long were you wearing it?" he said. His face looked solemn.

"Maybe a half an hour or so," I said. "But it felt like only a few minutes."

"Did you see anything when you wore it?"

"No."

"Are you sure?"

I didn't know how to answer. "I don't remember. It felt like a dream."

"A dream or a nightmare?"

"A bit of both, I guess. Maybe more of a nightmare."

The suit guy nodded to the other one. "It's a working model."

"Tell me, Barry, have you been having any visions since you wore it? Any residual hallucinations?"

Residual hallucinations? I didn't want to tell him that behind him the Phii Dek was playing with the little girl on top of a crate marked "explosives." "I have been…seeing things, yes."

"Would you indulge us, Barry, and describe what you are seeing?"

I pointed behind him at the Phii Dek and the little girl playing on the explosives crate.

"Well, right behind you there is the ghost of a little Thai boy whose mother drowned him in the toilet. He is playing with a girl around four years old who died in a similar manner. They have been following me around for the last hour or so. Right now he is flipping me off and making a slow jerking-off motion with his right hand and mouthing the words 'you are such a fucking- retard.'"

Which is exactly what he was doing.

Suit man number one walked me through a few different scenarios that I could consider as future possibilities. One involved me going back to the toupee's location and bringing it back while they held Nok hostage. Another scenario involved Vato, Nok, and me becoming the next act for the bukakke worm chair show. If the first option seemed daunting, the suit man reassured me by saying that there was a Soviet-era Mi-24 Hind helicopter parked nearby that would serve as my transportation – so I wouldn't need to again battle through the afflicted hordes.

"We had it flown in from Vietnam. It has fifty-seven millimeter rocket pods and a twelve point seven millimeter Gatling gun that will give you maximum reassurance in these trying times," he said in his infomercial voice.

I thought this would be my *Wizard of Oz* moment, where I'm given the answers to my endless questions. I expected this guy to explain it all. Why the outbreak had happened. Why the toupee had made me see into another dimension. Why the worms were causing us to evolve into monsters, and why consuming ridiculous amounts of drugs seemed to block their effects. I asked him these questions, and he either replied, "That's classified" or "Our people are still working on that." He did concede to respond to one of my questions about the toupee – primarily because that's what he was after. Maybe he felt if I understood that I would appreciate its importance and act as less of a douchebag.

"Are you familiar with remote viewing?" he said.

"Yeah, a little."

"Do you know its history?"

"Not really."

"Well, for a period of time the United States and the Soviet Union were conducting research into the paranormal. They enlisted psychics to predict certain events. They also employed these people to find missile silos and other targets using remote viewing. This effort had mixed results and was finally closed.

People involved in the project helped create the KH-32 reconnaissance hairpiece," he said.

For a while, we stared at each other in silence. I remembered that old line about *he who speaks first loses,* and tried not to ask any more questions. Then I saw the Phii Dek standing on top of the man's head and pantomiming the act of hanging himself from a noose and then doing the "River Dance" in his death throes. I broke the silence.

"So why the fuck am I seeing ghosts?"

"We are not certain. It seems to be a side effect of the hairpiece. It works by stimulating the right amygdala of your brain and inducing a state of temporal lobe epilepsy. This is what some researchers believe has caused people throughout history to have religious visions – visions of heaven, visions of hell, or, in your case, visions of ghosts."

"So you developed this thing to do remote viewing on whomever, and the side effect is that I am having hallucinations?" I said.

"I can't answer any more questions at this time. If you retrieve the hairpiece, I will try to answer more."

Then it was apparently the other suit guy's turn, because he lit me up for what seemed like an hour. He asked the same questions over and over, and never seemed satisfied with my answers. Chang got bored and left to watch his birthday party debauchery. The Phii Dek asked me in my mind if I wanted the suit guys to suddenly choke to death on their own tongues.

"Can we just wrap this up please?" I said.

"Did Yuri say anything about where he was going?"

"He said he was going to Siriraj Hospital to get a face transplant, and then he was coming to Pattaya."

Both of the suit guys were alarmed, perhaps even scared. "Are you sure he is dead?" number two asked.

"I didn't check his pulse or anything, but he collapsed in a ball of fire, which made him look pretty dead to me," I said.

The suit guys had a private chat. I heard them talking about contingency plans and about an operation or something like that. I wasn't really paying attention because the Phii Dek was now in the process of tapping on a Chechen's skin. He could see the worms swimming under the surface of the man's skin and tapped on it the way a kid would on a restaurant aquarium. The radio of one of the Chechens squawked, and he ran out of the room. A few moments later, I heard gunfire.

At first, there were just a few shots – then it was an onslaught. I could hear the shooting erupt into a full-on firefight.

"Wait here," one of the suit guys said.

The suit guys and the Chechens ran into the club. The music was still playing, and, looking through the door, I could see that Chang hadn't yet left his seat. I saw Nok sitting in a booth with a huge platter of food in front of her. I turned to Vato and told him to grab a shitload of guns and whatever else he could carry – which might not have been the best way to phrase it to him. When I ran into the club, I realized that the firefight was coming from the street. I grabbed Nok by the arm and, despite her protests, managed to pull her into the back room with Vato.

"There's gotta be a way out of here," I said, locking the door behind me.

We looked around, but saw no exits.

"What should we take?" I asked Vato.

"Whatever you want, homie. I'm good, dawg," Vato said, as he patted his backpack which seemed to be on the verge of busting open.

"What'd you get?"

"Oh, about a thousand hits of ecstasy, some blow, some China, a few gold bars – which are really, really heavy, and some hand grenades."

"How about something more practical?" I said, handing him a TAR-21 from one of the crates.

"It still has packing grease on it. And I don't even know how to work this thing, homes," he said.

The room was full of weapons – everything from GPMGs to RPG-7s – and knew what most of them were from playing "first person shooters." I had never served in the military. I had no idea how to feed a belt of ammo into a machine gun, or how to clean the grease off of the TAR-21. In frustration, I just wiped it off on my pants.

There were crates of ammunition and spare magazines, but I didn't know what kind of bullets to load in each gun. I didn't want to try ammo at random and risk a weapon jamming or blowing up in my hands. A handgun and a shotgun were the only weapons I had ever fired.

At a firing range, I had fired a couple of RPGs in Cambodia, but I was drunk at the time and couldn't remember anything afterwards. The Cambodian guy had charged me thirty dollars per rocket, and said it would be three hundred dollars to blow up a cow. I sort of remembered there were two parts to the rocket. There was some kind of green- or blue-colored fuse or booster, and the other part was the warhead. I looked around the room and finally found a few crates full of these. This room was an Idaho survivalist's wet dream, but I didn't know how to work any of it. In Texas, they'd execute me for my ineptness.

Vato, it seemed, had had male role models during his formative years, or had spent time in the underworld while working for Chang. He told me that a cretin had designed the RPG-7. Pulling the trigger only detonated the booster charge, which was screwed into the rocket's motor. G-forces were responsible for setting in motion a series of detonations that culminated in the warhead exploding upon impact. Vato had learned this from a former Taliban, who also showed him how to alter the rocket to make it an airburst round. The Taliban told Vato he had used this method to fire on coalition helicopters in Afghanistan. The cost for one of the most amazing and simple killing machines in the world was only three thousand dollars, and here we were – foregoing firepower so we could stuff our bags and pockets full of dope.

I handed Nok a 9mm Beretta, which looked ridiculous in her tiny brown hands. She put it down and sat on one of the ammo crates.

"What's wrong, babe?" I asked.

"I eating my food and you make me stop and–"

And blah blah blah. I ignored her and turned to Vato. "So what's the plan?"

Vato laid out a couple of huge lines of blow, inhaled one, and then offered me the rolled-up dollar bill. I waved it away. I wanted clarity, even if just for a few moments. Worms or no worms, I decided I wanted to spend my final hours or minutes with no chemicals in my system.

"You'll become one of them, you know?" Vato said.

"I know. If that happens, shoot Nok."

There was banging on the door. Then a voice. It was rougher than the last time I'd heard it. "Any of you sailors want to show a lady a good time?"

Vato was either shaking out of fear or from too much coke. It might have been a mixture of both. He looked around the room for a weapon. There was too much to choose from so he grabbed a mop that was propped up against the wall. With a few quick movements, I screwed the booster charge into the base of the RPG warhead and slid it into the tube.

"You can't use that in here, dumbass. You'll kill us all," Vato said.

He was right. I put the RPG down and picked up the Beretta.

"Is that you, Miss Hilton?" I said.

"Yes it is, boys."

I looked at Vato. "Your call, man."

"He's gonna kill us. I know it."

"Don't make me take the door off with the cute little Semtex panda I have in my purse. Open the door, boys. I want to show you my new look." Esmeralda said.

We waited in silence for what seemed like forever. It was Esmeralda who spoke first. "You want a cure for what's inside of you? How about for the baby growing inside of monkey girl?"

"What do you want from us?" Vato said.

Esmeralda just giggled. "I just want to show you my new face."

The Phii Dek appeared in front of the door and reached up for the lock. He flashed me his trademark diabolical smile. In his face, I could see something bubbling up. It was a collage of every psychopath and deviant he'd been in his previous lives. The mother who'd drowned him had done the world a favor. He would keep coming back again and attain a new incarnation, until he'd achieved his soul's purpose – whatever that was. Now that doorway was his birth through Nok. He would help us live, only so he could have life. That was the deal he offered.

"This is your only way out, fuckwad," the Phii Dek said. I nodded to him in agreement.

The Phii Dek unlocked the door and opened it. I could see into the club where Chang sat at his booth. His beloved Tiffany showgirls were with him. All of their eyes had been removed, leaving empty red sockets. A few of the Chechens groped their way around on the dance floor like sightless fish from the bottom of the ocean. When they turned to face me, I saw that their eyes were missing. Esmeralda stepped into the doorway. I stared at her feet trying to avoid eye contact.

"Hello, boys," he said. "How do you like the new me?"

I raised my eyes and took in the image. Esmeralda had changed his dress, and was now wearing a traditional Thai dancer ensemble. The skin on his legs and arms was covered in third-degree burns. Before my eyes could reach his face, I heard Vato gasp, then say, "Beautiful, Miss Hilton. Looking good."

I looked up at Esmeralda and blurted out some words before a micro-expression of disgust had a chance to cross my face. "Oh my God, can I have your autograph, Miss Hilton?"

The fire had melted the Paris Hilton impersonator mask onto his face. Bits of fat and pus bubbled up from where the mask had melded into his skin. I could smell the infection starting to grow, as bacteria multiplied by the billions in the Petri-dish-like climate. I needed to change the subject.

"What happened to everybody's eyes, Miss Hilton?" I said.

Esmeralda turned and looked into the club, and then turned back to us. "Oh, them? They don't need eyes anymore."

"Why you do that to them?" Nok said. I was surprised to hear her speak up.

"Because, my dear, the universe is not infinite. It has an edge, and what lies beyond it requires no eyes to see."

Vato and I both looked at Nok, then back at Esmeralda. "I don't think she's going to quite get that," I said.

"Arai na?" Nok said.

"Nothing, baby. This bitch is fucking nuts," I said.

Esmeralda's second set of lips hung loose as he spoke. "Where's the toupee, boys?"

My insult hadn't seemed to register.

"It's on the tollway between here and Bangkok," Vato said.

"Take me to it."

"Why do you want it so bad? What the fuck is that thing?" I asked

"Did you wear it?"

"Yeah. For a little bit."

"And what did you see?"

"All kinds of freaky shit. Like the little ghost of a Thai boy who, while we speak, is looking under your dress and pinching his nostrils closed because he says your ass is stinky," I said.

Esmeralda looked between her legs and waved to the Phii Dek. "He's cute. Is that his little girlfriend over there?" Esmeralda said, as she pointed to the ghost girl in the corner of the room.

"You can see them?"

"Of course I can. In answer to your question, the toupee allows you see everything that once remained hidden. Once you

133

have worn it, your sight shall never be the same. You, too, will no longer need eyes," Esmeralda said and held up a blood-covered soupspoon. "Shall I remove them for you?"

"Get the fuck away from me," I said and raised the RPG at her...I mean him. This seemed to make Esmeralda giddy. He held the spoon underneath his own eyeball instead.

"Did you know that your soul is a quantum computer? Or that your thoughts are physical? Our brain waves float along the Earth's magnetic field until they meet something that has the same frequency. The toupee mimics the field of what you are try-ing to observe, so that you are now on the same wavelength. Not just with one thing, but with everything."

"Yeah, well, I don't really understand any of that. Like I said, if you want the toupee, it's on the tollway," I said.

Esmeralda stepped back from the doorway. "Would you boys come with me, please? There's something special I would like to show you."

"Like what?" I said

"It's outside. Don't worry, I think you will like it."

I turned to Vato, "You wanna go?"

"Fuck no. He's acting all creepy and shit."

"He always acts creepy."

"Why don't we just shoot him? We've got a shit ton of guns in here."

"Because he walked past all the Chechens who were mega armed and managed to gouge out their eyeballs with a soup spoon. I don't even know if he's human," I said.

Vato and I looked at each other. He put down the mop and heaved on the backpack full of drugs. Then he leaned in and whispered to me. "If you get a clear shot, waste her with the

RPG. Shoot it at her, I mean, at his feet so it detonates. If you shoot *him* with it, the rocket will either pass through his body or just get stuck in there."

I picked up the RPG and Vato showed me where to find the safety catch. I was thinking of leaving Nok in the room and locking the door, and then I saw the Phii Dek standing behind her with his hands around her boobs. I picked up the 9mm and gave it to her.

"Honey, if something bad happens, kill yourself, okay?" I said. Suicide was the only solution I could envision. I saw the worms moving in her eyes, and what I thought was a large vein running through her forehead – until I saw it burrow underneath her scalp. She seemed out of it again.

"I'm waiting, boys. Don't make mamma come get you."

"Hang on, Miss Hilton," I said, then turned to Vato. "This is the end. I know it."

"It's all good, homie. It's been fun, man," Vato said and extended a bent elbow to me.

"Porno handshake?"

"Yep, porno handshake," he said.

The two of us bumped elbows then walked out into the club. Nok stood behind me with the Phii Dek and his little girlfriend holding her hands. I looked around the club…Chang and the Tiffany girls sat in their booth with eyes missing but weren't dead. They moved their heads as if following an object flying in the air. When I turned, I could see part of what they were "viewing" in my peripheral vision. As far as I could tell, it looked like a dude riding a giant dildo with wings.

"What in the fuck is that?" I said.

Esmeralda and the Phii Dek could both see what I saw.

"That's not a flying dildo, you retard," the Phii Dek said. *"It is a ghost called a Phii Kra Hung."*

"Oh, I thought that was a cock with wings and a dude was riding on it."

"Who you talking to, homie?" Vato said.

"Nobody."

"It is the spirit of a man who practiced black magic but did not follow its rules," the Phii Dek said. *"And that's not a dildo. It's a pestle, and those aren't wings. They are rice threshers. Holy shit, I can't believe my future father is such a colossal fuck-tard."*

I turned to the Phii Dek, "You know, if and when you are ever born, I honestly hope once again your mother drowns you in the toilet. I may even help."

The Phii Dek started to cry. It was a banshee's howl that pierced through my body and shot through every corner of my skull.

"I'm sorry," I said to him. The Phii Dek ran out through the front door of the club and onto the street. His little girlfriend trotted along behind. Before she left, she turned and waved.

"Sit down in one of the booths please," Esmeralda said.

Vato, Nok, and I took a seat in the only booth that didn't have a person sitting in it with his eyes scooped out. I saw the morose Chinese crooner cowering in a corner with the ping-pong ball girl. They still had their eyes, and, from what I could tell, they weren't infected.

"Do you have paper and a pen?" Esmeralda asked.

I felt my pockets. I still had the pen from earlier this morning. "I've got a pen, but no paper."

Esmeralda looked on the floor and spotted a bound stack of green Chinese takeout menus from a place called Chow Hai. Esmeralda picked up the stack of menus and giggled. When he did, the lips from the Paris Hilton impersonator mask jiggled and dripped pus. "Chow Hai means smelly cunt in Cantonese."

"You speak Cantonese?" Vato said.

"I just know the phrase chow hai."

I thought about this for a moment. "Wait, so the only phrase you know in Cantonese just happens to be the name of a restaurant on a menu, which happens to be lying at your feet at the exact moment that you need paper?"

"Apparently so," Esmeralda said.

I looked around the room. There was Chang, the Chinese gangster, sitting with two Tiffany showgirls, who stared (with no eyes) at a ghost that resembled a flying dildo. A sightless Chechen rebel felt his way around the room looking for something to use as a suicide method. The depressed Chinese crooner cowered in the corner with the torn-up-looking Thai woman whose job entailed shooting ping-pong balls from her vagina at a high velocity. Outside, I heard the screeching of a thousand undead monkeys and the screams of those they'd torn apart, along with the gunshots of hundreds of afflicted soldiers fighting for the right to live out a few more days of hedonism before the parasites inside their bodies transformed them into monsters.

"This isn't happening," I said.

Esmeralda smiled through his pus-filled lips. "What's not happening?"

"All of it. None of this is happening."

"And what makes you say that?" Esmeralda said.

"It's too fucking random. The menu. The parasites. Your face. The ghosts. It's all too random to be happening at once. Weird shit happens, yes, but not all at the same time. It's not normal."

Vato looked around the room as well. He nodded in agreement. "Yeah, it's like a collective hallucination from these parasites in our heads. The afflicted are just paranoid schizophrenic psychopaths or something."

We sat in silence for a long moment. Vato and I looked at each other and both spoke at the same time. "Drugs," we said.

"You boys do drugs? Drugs are bad for you, don't you know that?" Esmeralda said with his obscene giggle.

I thought back to when we'd met Esmeralda. He hadn't done any drugs. Who else hadn't? *The Mormon coolie*, I thought. *The CIA hires all of those Mormons as spies. He had to be one of them. Who else? The Chinese crooner and the ping-pong ball lady – they had to be one of them, too.* My mind traced the steps we had taken to get here. I tried to think of everything that had happened before Nok and I got to the hotel.

"Think about it," I said. "Thailand has the death penalty for drugs. A few years back, there were all these extra judicial killings of drug dealers. This is Thailand's way of getting rid of their drug problem. They put all the offenders in an isolated city like Pattaya and just let everybody kill each other."

Vato was starting to cry. "I knew it! Those fuckers!"

Esmeralda sat down in the booth and put his hand on Vato's knee.

"Calm down, boys. Shhhhhh. There, there now," Esmeralda said. "I'm going to tell you a story, Joel, and you are going to write it down. When we are finished, you shall see."

****

I wrote the history of the end of the world in the margins of Chow Hai Chinese food take-out menus. For my own ending, I would try to find stationery far more formal. I was to be Esmeralda's biographer. Every celebrity needs one, and Esmeralda would be no different. He insisted that there was no conspiracy to eradicate drug users – not yet, anyway. The parasites were pirates, sailing on the littoral waters of neurons and synapses. Since the very beginning, they had been with us. They slept and ate, knowing only what was food and what was not. Now they had awakened and only the very few could see them. The toupee had been built for a different purpose, Esmeralda said. The same way Viagra had been developed for heart patients, but as a side effect it gave people boners.

"The toupee was developed for remote viewing of military targets. The people who wore it claimed they had looked through other dimensions before the objective came into view. For many, it was journey through hell, or a vision of ghosts that walk within our world. Even when these people took off the toupee, they still had the visions. Needless to say, most of them went insane. The nonbelievers and scientists who had developed it attributed their visions to temporal lobe hallucinations. The test subjects were medicated, institutionalized, or involuntarily disappeared. Then we made contact with something that had been here all along. It was our first contact with an alien intelligence, and it was already inside our bodies. It wasn't long before the Army wanted it as a weapon."

"And you were one of the test subjects?" I said.

The sightless Chechen, who was feeling his way around, finally found an AK. He placed the barrel under his chin and pulled the trigger. A mass of black worms shot out of the hole in his head. There was little blood or brains.

"Did you see that?" Vato said

"Yeah, case in point. Why would that retard kill himself if the worms desired life?" I said

"Because men are expendable. One man can impregnate a hundred women. If there are too many men, a population will die off. The parasites need females to live," Esmeralda said.

The gunfire outside the club grew closer. I could hear shouting in several languages, as the troops outside seemed to be making a last stand by the door.

"How in the fuck did you get in here anyway?" Vato asked.

Esmeralda smiled through his extra face. "I had help," he said and left it at that.

Esmeralda's story began in prison – the one with the dark sobriquet, *The Bangkok Hilton.* His words were cryptic by design. I tried to avoid looking at his burned and disfigured face with its extra set of flapping lips – mainly because the drugs were wearing off. As he spoke, his voice normalized. Gone was the affectation of femininity. His voice was now almost self-conscious, as if he had become aware of how hideous he truly looked.

"Matter and spirit are the same," he said. "They differ only in their stage of evolution. First there is spirit, and then there is matter, then spirit rises again as the matter dies. It is no different than particles and waves. No different than water and ice. They are one thing in two forms. The shadows exist in the dark matter of the universe. They are in the void between thoughts. They exist in your reflection, as well as your shadows and dreams. The can see us. They wait only for us to see them."

"Yeah, once again, that's over my head," I said.

"Don't you understand yet? We can see them now, and they

know that we can see them. There is no longer a need for them to hide."

"So why were you in jail?" I said.

"I don't know. I woke up one day in prison. Whole chapters of my life were gone. I didn't know how I got there, or what I was in for. I asked no questions from the guards, as I was trying to figure out who put me in there, and who was being paid to watch me."

Esmeralda ordered me to write, and so I did. The gunshots outside started to die out – either because they were running out of ammo or the soldiers were getting eaten. I suggested opening the door and bringing the troops ammo, but Esmeralda would have none of it. I picked up my pen and began to write in between the descriptions of Peking Duck and Sexy Chicken Surprise. I listened to Esmeralda's story while my mind tried to figure a way out.

Esmeralda awoke in prison to the sounds of crying. It was a female voice, disconnected and full of static. Esmeralda stood up and stepped over several men with elaborate Khmer tattoos known as Sak Yant – the insurance policy of the Thai underworld, the bulletproof vests of the supernatural. The tattoos never seemed to keep them out of jail, though.

As Esmeralda neared the toilet, he saw a figure slumped over. A trail of blood and shit led to a mess of long hair. It was a woman's head, with her face stuck deep into the toilet. He listened as the head moved side to side making slurping sounds. It was licking the shit off of the sides of the bowl.

"Excuse me, Miss?" Esmeralda said.

The head stopped moving and a low growl emitted from its lungs. The figure shot up and did an about-face. It had the features of a beautiful woman – albeit, one who had smoked crack for many years. She was speaking to him. It was a metallic voice, scratchy, and full of static, as though he was hearing her through an old radio. Her image seemed projected on the background of the toilet. Not an apparition, but a projection from an old eight-millimeter film.

The beautiful crack-head face hovered – brighter now, revealing the blue veins running through her cheeks. The crow's feet around her eyes gave her some age, and black gums flashed when she smiled. She tilted her head back as she emitted a laugh –a disconnected laugh broadcast from another time. The projection moved towards him. Her nightgown opened to reveal a body composed of internal organs. She had no arms or legs, only the mechanical churning of her heart beating and lungs expanding. Shit was dripping from the edges of her mouth. Her guts did their job – processing food and leaving deposits of feces on the floor behind her.

Esmeralda stood motionless. He felt no fear – only a vague sense of acceptance. To be devoured by a Phii Krasue would be a suitable ending to his life. A brief image of his epitaph entered his mind and then was gone.

Esmeralda closed his eyes and waited for the end. So many times before, he had been denied this moment. He could smell the shit on her mouth and feel her breath on his face, as she grew closer. There was no sound, only the heaviness of her presence. Her tongue entered his mouth, drinking in his saliva. He choked as the tongue made its way past his tonsils and entered the long tunnel to his stomach. Esmeralda brought up a shank from his waistband and drove it into her face. Her jaw melted away as the blade cut its way through. He swung again and severed the tongue, which fell to the floor. A radio static scream came from somewhere deep inside of her. Esmeralda followed up with a few more blows, plunging the shank into the yellow orbs through which the Phii Krasue saw the world.

The eight-millimeter image flickered – grainier now. In her visage, he saw a house appear – an old, colonial French offering. The Phii Krasue turned and moved towards the open doors. The world around Esmeralda was now from another era. As she made her way outside, Esmeralda followed the Phii. This wasn't a home – it was a headquarters. Americans in spectacles and crisp, short-sleeved shirts loitered about. They were academic types, consultants to a war in progress. The Phii Krasue led Esmeralda up a magnificent staircase. Accompanied by more of the academics, men in Army formal descended the stairs but did not notice them. They spoke of logistics. They spoke the unmistakable lexicon of war

She led him down a hallway to a bedroom. The door opened, and for a time he wasn't sure what he was witnessing. It was not a scene of homicide. It was a scene of slaughter. A group of women brandishing machetes were dissecting a younger woman lying helpless on the floor. Without explanation, the young woman's story became known to Esmeralda. The Phii Krasue played a movie for him on the nebulous air that surrounded her – the young woman's screams serving as the soundtrack for the horrors of his soul. The women with the machetes knew the young woman's true identity. They had come to kill the demon that had taken the lives of their children. It was no accident that this had happened to five women in just one village. Esmeralda saw the eight-millimeter film of their late-night meetings. The group had determined the guilt of the one woman who held the demons traits. It was the young woman who lived alone and had been heard by passersby coughing and moaning in pain. The woman was known to dine on frogs. She could be seen at night with a light affixed to her head, catching them and snapping their necks.

The woman who limped with pain, who coughed incessantly, and walked sleepless at night fueled by a diet of frogs and excrement had all the qualities of a Phii Krasue. To kill her, they had to catch her in her human form, as she returned to the village after feeding on the blood of newborns.

The women approached the stilted home where the Phii Krasue lived. Machetes in hand, they waited in the shadows under her home. They held bottles of Jujube juice – the ghost's only weakness. While she was in human form, they would strike. The only other option was to destroy her body while the detached was wandering through the night. If the head returned home and couldn't find its body, it would die. None of the women were brave enough to venture out while the Krasue was hunting.

The beautiful woman never returned. Perhaps she knew of the conspiracy and moved to another village. Time went on, and rumors came of more newborn deaths from distant villages. Then came word that the Phii Krasue had met a farang and was living in a large home in Bangkok. Didn't the farang know he was in love with a demon? This farang was renowned in Southeast Asia for his intelligence and expertise. He and his organization could plan bombing raids in Laos, but he could not see the evil inside the woman he loved.

Esmeralda saw the images on fast forward: The group of women boarding a train, one applying for a job at the French mansion, opening the door at night for the others who hid their machetes in sarongs. The group stalking up the staircase while the young woman slept, and then to this scene of slaughter.

This was not a case of mistaken identity or local superstition. They had the right woman, and did what was necessary to protect their children.

As the group stabbed and hacked away with machetes, the young woman reached up and pulled down one of her assailants.

She locked her mouth onto her killer's, and rammed her tongue down her throat. The Phii Krasue in human form filled the woman's mouth with a jet of saliva, before her head dropped to the floor – mouth open and laughing. The saliva was a curse that all Phii Krasue gave to their killers. It would cause the woman she infected to carry on her legacy as another ghost, who would roam the countryside in search of more shit and babies to devour.

This was the Phii in front of Esmeralda – the one the spiritual parasites had infected. When he realized the gift the ghost was passing on to him, a tear welled up in Esmeralda's eye – because all Phii Krasue were women. Yes, a Phii only transferred its spirit to another woman. But this one had kissed Esmeralda, and had recognized his true gender. She'd seen the woman inside of him, unconcerned with what was between his legs. If the spirit knew Esmeralda's true nature, surely he'd chosen the correct path.

When the Phii turned to Esmeralda, the image of the French colonial home faded away. They were back in the Bangkwang cell, surrounded by snoring malefactors oblivious to the events around them. In a quiet voice, Esmeralda thanked the ghost, who turned and moved towards the toilet. Esmeralda followed her and watched as she buried her face in hole – taking in one last meal before she moved on. The static, old-radio voice spoke, beckoning him to join her. She would show him how to feed and how to move through this world. Esmeralda knelt beside the Phii, as her image faded away like the last frame of film in a projector. He was left alone with the sounds of the Jing Jok, making their music of kissing sounds to their paramours in the dark.

Esmeralda placed his hands on the sides of the toilet and looked down. This was a Thai-style toilet. A hole in the ground covered with the shit spray of a hundred dysenteric prisoners. He lowered his head and breathed in the odor. It was something he would need to get accustomed to if this was his new calling. Esmeralda extended his tongue and began licking the shit-encrusted sides of the bowl.

A hand grabbed the back of his shirt and pulled hard.

"What the fuck are you doing?" It was the voice of a fellow prisoner, a Brit who had been locked up for smuggling drugs.

Esmeralda stared into the brown mess of expelled tapeworms, and began to sob. He remembered flashes of hospital rooms and IV tubes, needles and two-way mirrors, men with clipboards making notations of the experiments at hand. Esmeralda's mind filled with a flood of images that left him unable to speak. He saw stacks of papers and area studies. He saw interrogations and tortures labeled as "interviews." Esmeralda saw himself in African shantytowns, Brazilian favelas, and Central Asian mountain passes. From what time period or in what conflict was anyone's guess. Images of guns...men wearing ski masks and brandishing knives...checkpoints and customs lines...packages taped to his body...he saw bodies turned upside down, and flayed alive by men who were professionals in the art of pain. He remembered one of them.

"I remember now," Esmeralda said to me. "Hang on a second."

Esmeralda put his head in his hands and was quiet. The troops outside banged on the front door and begged to be let inside.

"Maybe we help those people, na?" Nok said.

Esmeralda remained motionless. Pus dripped from his face and onto the table, forming a small pool that for some reason reminded me of the shape of Alaska. Vato and I looked at each other. He stood up and began walking towards the door.

Esmeralda turned his faces to the Chinese crooner. "Excuse me, do you know 'Girl from Ipanema'?"

The crooner nodded.

"Would you please sing it for me?"

The crooner seemed frozen. The banging on the door was getting more desperate, and Vato was cursing that the lock was jammed.

"Hello? Could you sing it for me, please?" Esmeralda asked in a gentle voice.

The crooner nodded and stood up. He shook as he walked to the karaoke machine and looked for the song. The ping-pong ball girl remained in the corner. Her eyes were closed and she appeared to be mumbling some kind of prayer.

"You remember what?" I said to Esmeralda.

The Chinese crooner found the song and hit play. Upon hearing the music begin, Esmeralda stood up and backed away from the table. He held his arms out to his sides and lowered his head melodramatically. For a moment, I thought he was about to *Vogue.*

The Chinese crooner began in his mournful voice, "Tall and tan and young and lovely, the girl from Ipanema goes walking, and when she passes, each one she passes goes–ahhh..."

Esmeralda brought his hands to the center of his chest and covered his heart. The pus was flowing from his face in a steady stream, and the Paris Hilton impersonator mask was slipping off. I looked at the puddle of pus forming on the floor. It took a moment to register, and I had to do a double take because it seemed Esmeralda no longer had any feet.

Esmeralda ripped open his dress as the Paris Hilton mask finally slid from his face. He no longer had a body. From the neck to the floor, Esmeralda was made only of entrails. A diseased-looking heart pumped with the fury of a Meth addict's in the center mass of intestines. I looked at Esmeralda's face. It had transformed into that of a beautiful blonde celebrity – a woman full of guile and seduction and a taste for newborns. The Phii Dek appeared behind Esmeralda and started laughing.

"Thanks, you little fucker," I said to the Phii Dek.

"What do you care? Esmeralda Krasue only wants what I want. It's what we all want," the Phii Dek said.

The Esmeralda Krasue opened her mouth. She had vampire-like fangs and a sharp proboscis for a tongue. She wagged the proboscis at me and let out a loud hiss.

"What the fuck do you want?" I said.

The Phii Dek stood next to the Esmeralda Krasue. He raised his hand and pointed at Nok. *"Mamma,"* he said.

The front door opened with a bang, and Vato came running into the room. As he saw the Esmeralda Krasue, he stopped in his tracks. Right behind him were about a half dozen Chechens who were bleeding and in near hysterics. One yelled something to another in Russian, which I gathered to mean "close the fucking door!" The sad Chinese crooner stopped singing and made a break for it before the front door closed, as "The Girl from Ipanema" played in the background.

The Esmeralda Krasue faced the Chechens and her disembodied head floated towards them. The Chechens could see her, for they seemed freaked out. The Esmeralda Krasue stuck out her proboscis and plunged it into the neck of a Chechen. Vato ran over to our table and grabbed his bag of drugs.

"Priorities dude," he said to me.

I took Nok by the arm and stood up from the table. We ran to the back room with the weapons but the door shut before we could get inside.

I turned and looked at the Phii Dek. *"Open it you little shit,"* I said.

"After," the Phii Dek said.

"After what?"

"After we take that out of her," he said, pointing to Nok's belly.

The Phii Dek stood in the middle of the room. From the necks of the Chechens, the Esmeralda Krasue drank blood, which traveled through her intestines and left giant piles of excrement on the floor below her. It seemed Vato had developed a thing for mops, because he grabbed another one and hit the Esmeralda Krasue across the jaw. In response, the Esmeralda Krasue opened her mouth and vomited a jet of shit onto Vato's face. Something about it made me snicker.

"I want life and Esmeralda wants the placenta. After I am born, we will both have what we desire," the Phii Dek said.

Nok and I backed into the corner with the ping-pong ball lady, who was still cowering and mumbling her prayers. Vato ducked another jet of excrement and ran over to us. I looked around. The RPG was near the booth. So was the 9mm.

"You have a gun?" I asked Vato, who was wiping shit from his eyes.

"Just some grenades in my bag."

"Well, pull them the fuck out and frag this skank," I said.

Vato opened his bag and started rummaging through it. "Sorry, homes, they're on the bottom."

The few remaining Chechens sprayed the Esmeralda Krasue with automatic gunfire. The bullets passed through her body of entrails and hit the wall above us. I ducked down next to the ping-pong ball lady and smelled something stinky.

"Got em dude," Vato said, as he pulled out grenade after grenade.

That was when I had what was arguably the second worst idea I'd had all day.

"Nok, can you translate for me?"

"Arai na?"

"Tell ping-pong ball lady to do something for me," I said and held up a grenade.

Nok tapped the ping-pong ball lady on the shoulder and spoke to her in the Isaan dialect. The woman opened her eyes and looked around in terror. She seemed to comprehend what we were saying because she opened her legs and lifted her skirt.

"What are you doing, dude?" Vato said.

"Getting us out of here," I said, as I pulled the pin on the grenade. I held the handle down and looked the ping-pong ball lady in the eyes. She nodded at me as though she understood what I wanted.

I released the handle on the grenade and put it inside the ping-pong ball lady's well-worn and muscular vagina. "Frag out!" I shouted.

The ping-pong ball lady used a mixture of muscle contractions and vaginal flatulence to expel the grenade with tremendous force. The sound of her beaver burp filled the room as the grenade sailed home.

The Phii Dek and the Esmeralda Krasue looked at me for the split second before the explosion. Since I'd been raised on a steady diet of action movie one-liners, I regretted not having something witty to say. The grenade landed in the mass of entrails underneath Esmeralda's neck and lodged just beneath her heart. There was a one-second delay before it exploded. I used that time to hide behind Nok.

The grenade erupted in a fireball, which engulfed the Esmeralda Krasue and everything within a fifteen-meter radius. That included us. It was over in an instant. My eardrums felt as though they were shattered. I didn't feel heat from the blast or any shrapnel piercing through my body. I only felt the warm splatter of blood coming from the ping-pong ball lady's neck as her arteries sprayed my face. The room was on fire and full of smoke. When I opened my eyes, I saw the Phii Dek and his little girlfriend standing in front of us with their arms outstretched. They had prevented the shrapnel from killing us. The ping-pong ball lady had not been so lucky.

It took a few minutes to regain our equilibrium and shake the cobwebs from our brains. The Phii Dek and his little girlfriend got down on the floor and snuggled under Nok's arms. Nok could see them, and she stroked their hair in a loving manner.

"I thought you wanted to kill us," I said to the Phii Dek.

"No, you needed to rid the world of evil. I knew only you could do it," the Phii Dek said.

"Yo, homie, lets go grab one of those Jet Skis and get out of here," Vato said.

"How? The streets are crawling with those things," I said.

"We are safe now, there will be nothing to fear," said the Phii Dek.

"What happened to Esmeralda?"

"She went to another place. This was not her world. She was born into the wrong one, and now she can go be happy," the Phii Dek said. He was starting to sound like Nok.

"Listen, it's quiet outside. I think it's time to go," Vato said.

We stood up and walked through the wreckage of the night-club. There was no remnant of Esmeralda to be seen. Body parts from the Chechens were strewn around the room. A hand sat in a flowerpot with its middle finger up, and a pair of lips landed around the neck of a beer bottle. Vato opened the door, which led onto Walking Street. There were bodies everywhere. I could see no traces of the worms in them.

"It doesn't look like they're infected," I said.

"You killed the main host. Now all of them will leave the bodies."

We proceeded down Walking Street towards where we'd left the Jet Ski. There were survivors emerging from hiding like insects after the rain. Nok held the hands of the Phii Dek and his little girlfriend as they trotted along next to her.

"We need to find the toupee," I said to Vato.

"What in the fuck for?" he said.

"Because it's dangerous. That apocalypse hair hat will destroy the world if the wrong person gets hold of it. I get the feeling that the two suit dudes are going to try and find it."

"It's over, man. I'm going home," Vato said.

I stopped walking, and Vato continued on. I looked at Nok and asked if she wanted to go with me. She said she would, and for that reason I told her not to do it. I told her to go home to her mom's house and that everything would be fine.

"Excuse me, sir, do you need a ride?" said a voice from behind. I turned and saw the Mormon coolie, who now had a tuk-tuk instead of a rickshaw. He looked as though he'd come through the ordeal unscathed.

"Yeah, take her home," I said.

"And where is home?"

"Sisaket. It's a long drive. Consider it part of your penis penance," I said.

"Very well then."

I didn't hug Nok because I felt that would be saying good-bye. I handed her some money and told her I'd call her soon. Then I turned and started walking north.

"Where are you going, sir?" the coolie called out.

"North, towards Bangkok."

"Hop in, sir, it's on the way."

Might as well, I thought. I got into the tuk-tuk with Nok and the ghost children, and we headed out. The thousands of afflicted that had stormed the gates had trampled the barricade to Walking Street. We drove through the debris and hit the main road. I looked to my left towards the beach and could see a figure on the ocean. It was Vato on the Jet Ski, with his giant bag of drugs for a passenger. He raised his arm in what appeared to be a thumbs up. We drove parallel to each other until the road split away and he faded from sight.

"What happened to crazy lady?" Nok asked.

It seemed too complicated to explain in my Tarzan Thai, but I gave it a try. "Lady who turn into Phii Krasue and have ugly hair thing on her head was same lady who number one big boss worm. Ugly hair thing on lady head make so she can talk to worm, and I think Army make the ugly hair thing to do something else, but it make people go crazy and see Phii. She the number one worm lady and when she die, all the worm die, too," I said. Then I added, "Kao jai mai?"

Nok nodded out of courtesy, "Ka, kao jai," she said, even though she had absolutely no idea what I was talking about.

I saw a cat emerge from under a car. It was the first animal I had seen in some time. I told the Mormon coolie to stop the tuk-tuk, and I walked back to where I'd seen it. The cat came up to me and rubbed himself on my leg. I stared out into the world and saw so many – the rise and fall of shadows to and from this world. Anyone that has chosen this life will hear their call, and will have found themselves confused and misled by them since birth. I see them now, and know how much more work there is for me to do.

I picked up the cat, and it purred with pleasure in my arms. The cat blinked at me with that smug look that means they trust you, and if there is anything in the feline emotional cosmos that equates with love, the cat offered me that as well. Together, we watched the shadows fall to Earth. By the way the cat's eyes moved, I knew he could see them too.

We drove north for quite some time. People who had once been sleepers or afflicted I saw stumbling around as if they had the worst hangovers of their lives. One man had already started to cook food for people at a roadside stand. It wouldn't be long before the markets opened up and the delicious fragrance of diesel smoke choked the air. There would be the smell of lemongrass and fish sauce, and the warm smiles of the Thai people, and the wind would carry with it everything I loved.

About the Author

J.D. Villines was born in Chicago, and has worked as a special effects makeup artist, a zookeeper, a bounder, a Muay Thai instructor, and a roadie for punk bands. He divides his time between Bangkok and Los Angeles.